SARĒ MARĒ

■ **S. K. Walker** came to Britain in the late 1950s from the Indian subcontinent. She studied at Nottingham and Manchester Universities.

PANDORA PRESS FICTION ORIGINAL

SARĒ MARĒ

S. K. Walker

London

First published in 1987 by
Pandora Press (Routledge & Kegan Paul Ltd)
11 New Fetter Lane, London EC4P 4EE

Set in 10½/12½ pt Garamond
by Witwell Ltd. Liverpool
and printed in Great Britain
by the Guernsey Press Co. Ltd.
Guernsey, Channel Islands

British Library Cataloguing in Publication Data

Walker, S.K.
Sarè Marè.
I. Title
823 (F)   PR6073.A41/

ISBN 0-86358-169-2
0-86358-170-6 (pb)

CONTENTS

PART ONE

PART ONE

In a far off village in the Punjab surrounded by fields, trees and cattle-strewn dusty roads live a Brahmin family. The village is called Sarē Marē which means 'death to all'. No one knows why it was named thus, perhaps because of its heroic deeds in the deep past. It is predominantly a farming Sikh village; there has always been a high recruitment to the army and a glorious record of service in the two world wars.

The Brahmin family are in a minority. They are misfits as they do not follow the traditional pattern of prayer and worship and, worst of all, they educate their daughters. The wife does not practise purdah (covering the face) and the daughters are allowed to roam around unchaperoned.

In this strange and contradictory atmosphere of rebellion and conformity Asha, the middle child, listens to the stories of the grown-ups – from her mother, from her grandmother, her elder sisters and other people. The stories of her mother's marriage, of women and roles within the extended family colour her consciousness from early childhood. She listens enraptured to the story of how her mother came to be married as they walk together to visit her family. The road is dusty, the sun is setting and Asha is weary and thirsty. In the pink haze and the slow tinkling of cowbells, the story assumes a magical, dream-like quality, and in the hypnotic telling of the tale she enters into her mother's experiences as if she was there.

MOTHER

I was only ten then and your father fifteen when we were married. I was a child, I did not know what was happening. My father said my husband was handsome like the full moon: he had white teeth like a row of pearls and his eyes were lit with candles. I was a child much given to playing with rag dolls and I made them all – such lovely dolls. You ask your father about the dolls I made on my honeymoon. I made them out of bright-coloured rags and dressed them with banana leaves! Out of broken glass bangles I made jewellery, bangles, bracelets, earrings and necklaces, and I made plaits for them out of real hair. They looked so real that I thought they could walk. It is a long time ago but how clearly I remember it all.

Yes, that was a grand wedding I had. My father was a rich landowner and even had a sugar mill – he spilt his riches over me. I was the eldest child and motherless so he did his best and it was a lavish affair. There were all kinds of sweetmeats, all made with real butter, and how they were arranged into mock stables, sky high! One hundred and forty men at the wedding party stayed for a whole week and were fed so well that they could not stand the sight of food for months. It was all fun and I did not know what was going on. I was happy and danced and flitted from one end of the room to the other.

My aunt was angry and told me to stop singing in case my inlaws heard me. But it was so nice, the whole house lit up with earthen lamps from end to end, and I was a mere child of ten. They can't afford weddings like that now: people don't have the means and the Mithai does not taste the same as it did then.

I remember how I was loaded with gold from head to toe. I must have carried pounds of it around me. It sounds funny now to think of the old customs. A woman was no woman if she wasn't weighed down with gold like a donkey. I had six sets of earrings in each ear. No wonder my lobes have split in two, but then I did not know or

4

care what was happening to me or my ears. I was only a child and did as I was told. I had a pair of bracelets with inset bangles and they were two pounds of solid gold. You can't find gold like that now. Its colour was of the fire – rich, burning yellow. When you saw a woman with all her wedding jewellery, why she could have been lit up from head to toe. Yes, there's no gold like the old gold I used to have!

I remember the morning when the sun was hot and the sky was a clear blue, and all the acacia trees were covered with yellow gold, laden with blossom. I was woken up by my aunt at midnight: there was another woman there and I did not know what was happening. Despite my loud protests and shrieks they bathed me with fragrant rose water, washed my long hair and combed it, and then braided it tightly into a hundred little plaits, weaving them into an intricate pattern, and into this pattern they wove a most uncomfortable tower – it was called Chowk and it hurt me so much that I cried. I pulled and tugged at it but it would not budge and only dug into me and hurt me more. I heard people bustling, hustling, jostling and running on the clear moonlit night. And then I heard the drums beating and a thousand shahnais playing echoingly, piercingly, mournfully together – there were the drums, the beenas, the sitars and tablas too. I was wide awake and running like a mad child in the courtyard with nothing on but this tower on my head.

I wanted to flee and see the source of all this music but my aunt and this other woman whom I had never seen before chased me into a corner. I was then dressed in a red velvet Shalwar Kameez embroidered with gold, and felt proud like a queen. But the shalwar was far too long. It kept slipping and slithering on the floor, though my aunt tied it twice after doubling it around the waist, and I looked like a very untidy, fat parcel. It was all so strange and dream-like – my sleeves were pinned into position, my face was smeared twice with thick red paste and then I was covered with a thick red veil until I could not see anything or touch my nose or see my toes. I let out a scream and struggled to free myself but it was all too late. I was carried down to where the sounds came from and where the drums were beating. I don't know what happened during the rest of the night, I must have fallen asleep while sitting on the wedding altar.

Anyway, when I woke up, I was on a mat in the company of my aunt and the sun was already high up in the sky. It was very hot and the sky was a clear blue, and all the acacias in the distance were loaded with yellow gold just like me.

I liked making dough balls for the chapattis, and as usual I went to make them in the kitchen. I was busy with this work in the middle of the day when this other woman called and told me to get ready. I was not given much time or maybe I did not know how best to use it. I had such a lot of pretty silk clothes to choose from, but all too big for me. Of course, now I know that my father-in-law had wisely instructed the tailor to make them longer and bigger so that they would fit me when I was a grown woman. Anyway, I was helped by my aunt to dress as usual. I heard the tinkling of bells, the heavy footfalls, and I knew it was a bullock cart. I ran to see it but was again stopped by this other woman. My face was covered and veiled ritualistically. Thus I was led blindfolded to my fate in this carriage.

When the woman kindly removed the veil from my eyes, I saw that on all sides the carriage was covered with tinselled curtains. I had a peep at the bullocks and they were garlanded with marigolds and rows of delicate little bells hung around their necks. They were beautiful. I heard the muffled sobs of my aunt and saw tears in my father's eyes. Perhaps he wished my mother was there to bid me farewell on this sunny day – the day of my wedding. But then I could not understand the complexities of human relationships and the sorrow at my near departure. I felt so happy as I gazed at my beautiful clothes and bright, shining bangles. I could not remember my mother – or mourn for her even if I wished to. She died a long time ago when I was a child, and only now sometimes I see a face, a round pretty face, with wide, gentle, black, sorrowful eyes, looking over me, and I know she is my mother. I cannot say if it is fancy on my part or if it is the face of my mother as I saw it dimly a long time ago.

I was told off for not showing any sorrow or regret at leaving my father and my aunt and going away forever to my husband's land. The woman kept whispering, weep, weep. But I did not understand the full meaning of what was going on, I was only a child of ten. I was bewildered and surprised at my father's behaviour. Why should he cry when he himself has brought this carriage for me? Why should my aunt sob when she herself has helped me to dress in these lovely clothes and fine jewels, and has told me to be good and respectful to the people I was going to meet? I did not know then that it meant for me a farewell to the surroundings and the wide open fields in which I had played, and the meadows in which I had danced and collected flowers.

It was very hot on the way and I felt sick. The road was bumpy and unending. I had a headache. Also for many days my diet had been sweetmeats, since I had never seen such a vast array of delicacies. Now I was paying for my ignorance and greed. I vomited all over the beautiful carriage. They had to stop the journey midway when I threw a tantrum and demanded my dolls to play with. Now, it all seems so ridiculous, I can laugh and cry to recall the past. Still, it must have been an embarrassment to the woman who went with me because I was not at all well behaved and would not stop crying. It took us a long time to reach my husband's village; it seemed as if the journey would never end. Night came. I slept in the lonely carriage with my head on this very patient woman's knee. I dreamt that the carriage was going down and down into this very dark pit. Now it was going round and round, revolving faster and faster around the dark pit, and was about to fall in it at any moment. My arms and legs were very sore and my eyes were red with tears, dust and exhaustion. When we were very near the village the woman who was looking after me seemed upset and asked what had happened to my hands. I said, nothing, it was only a bit of dried dough. I suppose nobody had examined my hands and told me to wash them. I must have looked a sight with my hands and arms encrusted with dried-up dough. They were caked right up to my elbows.

She told the driver to stop when he saw a pond. And there was a pond just outside the village gates. We alighted to wash my hands, but the dough had stuck to them like glue and dried hard. It must have taken half an hour before it was a soft enough consistency to be washed off. The water in the pond was green and buffaloes were being bathed in it. It was one of those ponds you find in every village which serves so many useful purposes, from washing clothes to watering the beasts, and the children bathe, swim and play in it. Turtles swim about in it, frogs, snakes, wasps and dragonflies live and love in it. Now it helped me to wash my doughy arms and hands and make me respectful.

Mother-in-law Palika rushed out with a jug of water and poured it on the wooden sills of the house. She blessed 'the bride' with sesame seeds and rice, scattering them all around me, and then took me in, full of loud innuendoes and eulogies. Soon the little sitting room was crowded with swarms of women and children. The children were carried astride generous hips with their stubby legs dangling on each side as if riding horses. The exciting atmosphere was affecting them too so they kept squirming, shuffling and crawling beside 'the bride' as if they were a bucketful of earthworms.

This other woman who was now identified as my nurse told me to touch these ladies' feet as a sign of respect. I did not much care to, but did as I was told. My mother-in-law was a stout, middle-aged woman. Although she was fat, she carried her shoulders very straight, and sat bolt upright. She had a mulish look about her. You could tell that she was a strongwilled woman. When she spoke her voice was harsh and grating – she even sounded like a mule – and she had a piercing, intense gaze with chilli-pepper eyes. She wished to know if I wanted anything to eat and I shook my head. I was like a little frightened dove in this dark, anonymous room with dark, sinister doors all heavy, handmade and carved. The small windows and the door frames were covered with garlands of mango and Jamun leaves. The walls were covered with the imprints of hands dipped in rice flour as this is the custom to celebrate auspicious occasions. I was told to sit on a very high bed which served as a sofa. It had an ivory headboard and huge mirrors were stuck in the middle of ivory. Wherever I turned and looked I happened to see myself. I was flushed red and the ornamental tower sitting on my head zoomed up and down as I shook my head! It was all so strange, in a strange house with strange people. I could not contain my anxiety and distress any longer. So I let go and gave yell after yell of piercing agony and terror as if I was shut away in a cage or put in a pen.

THE MOTHER-IN-LAW PRONOUNCES

'Son, my poor son! Your wife does not like our food. She will not eat a thing or speak. She comes from a high and mighty family! Our food does not come up to her standards, I suppose. My poor little child! Your wife is wild! She tears her bedsheets and her eyes are red with anger. God have pity on us. Doomed was the day when I approved of your marriage! She is so untrained, she will have to be tamed!'

'She is young, Mother, she doesn't know about life,' says the son.

'Not young enough to learn about it, my son,' answers the mother.

THE MOTHER-IN-LAW ORDERS

'Here is some corn, and here is your stone handmill. Come, come, my daughter, do something useful. And after you have ground the corn bring the flour to me. I will test it to see that it is ground fine.'

THE BRIDE LAMENTS

'My hands are soft and they were never meant to do such work, and my arms are stiff and aching. My heart cries when I hear the children playing in the street, and I wish to run away to join them. My hands are now blistered and red hot, and pinpricks of pain and throbbing pierce my weary soul. I wonder, if I asked my father to send me some money, would they stop making me do this horrid mill work?'

THE MOTHER-IN-LAW PERSISTS

'Have you finished grinding, my daughter? Not too bad, though your flour is rather coarse. It will get better. Now, come and help me with this heap of cotton. I want to turn it into cottonwool, and then I shall buy you a pretty little spinning wheel with bells. The spinning wheel would go round and round and you shall learn to sing all the spinning songs and be merry.'

THE BRIDE CRIES

'O God, the misery of my life! This wretched spinning wheel never breaks. I spin with my heart's blood and groan. I make a song of sorrow and sing it with its droning, O Wheel! – O Silken Black Crow, sitting on the edge of the verandah, go tell my father how sad his daughter is. I cannot read or write, my misery can only spin and multiply with the thread of the cruel Wheel.'

'Mother, mother, I am tired, sore and hungry, can I go to my bed and rest?'

'No, daughter, you must finish your pile of cotton before you go. Your sisters-in-law have already finished theirs. You are so clumsy and slow!'

(She knew not of love but fear. She dreaded the approach of her husband. The years went by and with each passing year, her fear changed into slow attachment and love. From time to time the mother-in-law wanted gifts, money and gold and these were delivered to her. Once when she had gone on a rare visit to her father a plot was hatched to get rid of the bride. A mere barber was sent to fetch her home and it was assumed that if she refused to come she would be left there forever. But her father was wise and he understood this move, swallowed his pride and sent mother back with the mere barber.)

THE MOTHER-IN-LAW ACCUSES

'Son, my darling son! You are running away from me. Your wife has worked her sorceries upon you and bewitched you. She has snatched my baby from me. She is a witch with shining black hair and the eyes of a venomous snake. Don't go away from me – your home, my son, or at least, do not take her with you.'

'Your hair is like silk,' says Raju, 'and your eyes like a frightened doe, and do not be afraid of me for we are married. I shall build you a palace of gold and buy you a cow whose milk is sweet like honey, and we shall have seven sons!'

'Mother, you are a foolish woman,' says Raju! 'You are jealous of my Jaya! She is a simple woman with a heart of gold and I intend to take her with me!'

'Son, leave me her jewellery at least, since I am afraid of foreign parts. There will be thieves and robbers and your bride is so trusting!'

'I do not wish to give away my jewellery. My father gave it to me and without it I feel naked and ugly,' protests Jaya.

'Don't argue, you silly fool,' says Raju. 'Give all the bangles, bracelets, rings and necklaces to your mother.'

'I won't,' protests Jaya, 'they are mine.'

'Give or I shall hit you … ' shouts Raju.

'I won't,' retorts Jaya.

'Then here … give,' Raju uses his hands and fists to acquire obedience.

Years have flown by and I wake up to find myself an aged woman. Youth never came to me for I was busy with the drudgery of life and bearing children. A wonderful family I had, and then there was Ramu – the most beautiful child you ever saw! Happy and healthy, he played from morning till dawn. He was full of life and beautiful. His face was like a half-open lotus flower, and his eyes were wide and dark, and he sang all day. He grew to be five years old and then he was snatched away from me. It is very painful to recall it now. He was playing in the morning and passed away at sunset in an instant. I was foolish and ignorant, and your father was right when he said that I did not know how to care for him. At least that's what he always said. Ramu was my first child and most loved too. That boy! I knew all along he wouldn't last. He was too good for this world. Then I heard stories from other women in the street that he was killed by witchcraft practised by a jealous woman. Of course, I believed it all. There are such things in the world! Don't laugh, my child. People are not all good. Some are so petty and small-minded that they get jealous and try to put an end to one's happiness. Unlucky me, I was away that night at Karmo. My friend told me that at 8 pm that night she saw a blazing object like a meteorite enter Ramu's bedroom window and take his breath away with it. He gave one single scream, and then passed away, and that was the end of him.

So we moved to another district, far away. And God, it was a dirty place, all infested by rats and mosquitoes. This was the place where your elder sister Rajee died. It was only six weeks after the death of her brother.

She was a happy child, much loved by her father and Ramu. The poor girl lost her will to live when he died. She felt his death most. Even now I recall clearly how every night when the wind swept by the window shutters, they fluttered, and the wind and the monsoon rain lashed their full fury on the doors of our poor house, she would ask, 'Where is Ramu? You think he will come back tonight?' Poor child, God have mercy on her! As I recall her waiting and longing for her brother something happens to me and I go insane. That is how your sister died: she pined away quietly in her father's lap without a sound. And he kept reading her a story while the poor child lay dead! Yes, I had my share of sorrows. After their deaths I went through a state of decline and inertia. I did not eat anything for days and only thought of joining my children. Then I had pneumonia but somehow lived through it. I dragged my body for a whole year; I was so weak that my feet seemed too heavy for me and my legs were lead weights. To make matters worse your grandmother started to poison your father's ears against me, and she was forever telling him to take on another wife. Such is the unhappy fate of a woman who cannot produce sons. Nobody wants to see her in case her misfortune is catching.

MOTHER-IN-LAW CONSPIRES

'Your wife would never produce a son, my son. I think you ought to remarry. A son is the hope of a Brahmin and without a son you will not enter the kingdom of heaven. Listen to your mother. There's time yet. You have a good job and property, your hair is still black, so why not marry again? I know you are fond of Jaya but she is too old to produce a son. It is a shame, but remarry, my unlucky son!'

MOTHER LAMENTS

'My weatherbeaten house is crumbling fast. So far God has not shown his mercy on this house and we are all getting old. Many summers come and many summers go, yet something precious is missing from life! In autumn, leaves swirl, curl and whirl from door to door. They are like beggars. They are old and yellowing. Their skins are sallow and wrinkled. Some of them are diseased, pierced by thorns. Their blood has all been sucked away by cruel nature. Yes, they are like old, crippled, leprosy-stricken beggars. They come empty-handed with their begging bowls and are pitilessly turned away at closed doors. I am like old dead leaves, like an old beggar, with my empty lap of a begging bowl. I hear the frogs croak in the rain. Their endless cries keep me awake at night and make me restless. Their croaking is not of joy but a harbinger of sorrow, of dolefulness, of despair, and of drowning in the abyss of life. The water in the street rises. It reaches the house. It laps at the door and then enters the bottom stairs. The furniture floats in it and is mud coated. The crops are all ruined once again and the houses fall.

In how many seasons have I seen these sights again and again? The sky is once again a mass of inky cloud which shrouds it from all sides. I hear the thunder. It is like a warring drum beat in the distance getting ever louder and harsher. It is like King Ashoka's armies marching to conquer the kingdom of Kalinga. And the lightning – it pierces the sky and shatters the clouds in a million pieces to be joined again instantly – made whole by the seamless needle of invisible hands. I hear the spring creeping. Creeping silently. Coming closer at the dawn of each morning. I smell its faint smoky smell and unfathomable sweetness. The trees in my courtyard are budded. My margosa tree dances, bathed in a white fragrance, moonwashed, its tender pink saplings dancing in the morning breeze. The shisham leaves are tiny. They appear shy as if they wish to disappear again in the bark and the branches. And the peepul at the edge of the pond looks at itself admiringly in the mirror, watching the tender pinkness of its leaves reflect in the morning sun. The bohar, the keekar and the berri are all clothed in the softest of greens. But in my heart and in my lap there is an unexplained emptiness never to be filled again. I, the mother of all daughters, have no son.

Asha reflects: I knew a boy once. Unwanted child. Uncared for, he died before my very eyes. Should I call my land the doomed land of ungrateful sons? Your men are lazy, feckless and cruel. Your daughters are always haunted by an unyielding fate, and have learnt to suffer silently. His mother was a foolish young woman who ran away from home and paid the price for breaking with tradition. Why did she run away?

One does not ask such questions.

She was sold into slavery and changed masters many times, and each time her price went down. Till it was the turn of this devil incarnate with a pitted face and one staring, cruel eye. He was so ugly that no woman would normally look at him. But he could afford to buy a woman – a fallen woman who had already been dispensed with by society. He made her work all day in the fields as soon as the hapless woman moved into his house. When I saw her again after the holidays she had already gone stark, staring, raving mad. She did not show any concern for the child. I stole some food for the boy – dried milk – and took it to the boy with white, staring, frightened eyes of death and despair. And the agony of it – I saw the mother snatch the milk away and drain it quickly herself. The child kept whimpering and crying and then all was silent. Should I have been angry with her? I did not know of her pain, oppressed by men, powerless, she moved about like a zombie in a trance. The child had a dirty cloth tied round his face and the mother removed it one day to let me see his sores. Half his face and ear were eaten away by maggots; he was already death personified. A child does not forget pain and sadness easily and cruelty is etched forever in its heart. I always remembered that no one cared for his crawling, festered head and face while the mother was forced to sit inert, like a statue, powerless, and saw it all. No one reproached the man for he was a landowner and was free to exploit women and murder children. He still kept the Izzat (male honour) which the woman lost by stepping out of a system which protects the strong and destroys the weak. Don't ever forget he was a son too! There are millions like him dying of neglect and cruelty.

'My son is a gift', cries mother. 'A gift descended upon my lap, bestowed by the kind Gods from heaven, and an answer to all my prayers. I hoped that one day I would be given a son, and I am lucky – to see this day! Thank you God, for your mercy, and when he is ten, I shall go barefooted to the Great Mother Ganga who is so kind to us, the Sinners!'

MOTHER

I grew up in the rice country. Of course, the best rice in the Punjab comes from there. Even now, whenever I go home, my father always gives me a load of rice. It is not like this Manjaki area. The Manjaki has mean people, right up to their backbones. There is a saying that they don't waste their spittle even. Why, they rub it on their hands to toughen them. But I came from a generous background. That's one of the reasons why I am so free. Anyway, I don't see the use of owning something if I can't lend it to my neighbour who has need of it. I don't care for possessions now. Though, when I was young, it was hard to forget when I lost all my gold. And beautiful sets of bangles and necklaces I had too. I used to have a ring for my thumb – it was a big ring with a mirror set in it. My mother-in-law swallowed it all. She never handed it back to me when she took it away from me on the pretext of safe-keeping. I was young then and did not know the minds of people. When I see my rings, necklaces, bracelets being used by her favourite son's daughters-in-law, it burns me up. It brings all my past bitterness back, so that I could cry and howl and hit anyone in sight. I really hated your grandmother then.

Neighbours come and listen to this old tale consolingly enough and then depart.

'Never mind Jaya,' says one. 'God has given you a son. You never know what he will become when he grows up. Now, can you lend me five rupees?'

Father says our mother is foolish and he is right. 'Never a borrower nor a lender be,' he says. She would never get the money back. Instead she has a quarrel. 'What did I tell you, Asha? Your mother is foolish, illiterate and ignorant,' says father.

'Mother, father has said that you are foolish, illiterate and ignorant.'

'Did he indeed. What did he do with the precious money he earned, I ask you? Most of it went to pay his father's debt. What did he gain? His land is going to waste through lack of care and his brothers are enjoying all he had in that village. His house, his shop, his land are all theirs and he has the audacity to tell you that I am foolish.'

'Asha's father, what have you been saying against me to the children? Answer me, don't just grin. The children have lost the little bit of respect they had for me. It's all your doing, you ape, you brute, you have wasted my life, and I slaved for you all those years!'

A terrible, uproarious battle ensues. The brass pots crash to the ground, milk spills over the floor, and father slaps mother in a most cruel manner.

Sobs fill the smoky room, they reverberate, they echo, and go back to their source with hiccups. Some sobs choke, others stay stuck, others croon like a dove in pain, and others howl out loud. Mother's pain stills the house and sickens us all.

Father has no pity, no mercy, he keeps grinning and repeating he is right.

'Leave me, if you wish; I will manage without you. Asha, tell your mother to pack her bags and leave. She is a useless, wasteful bitch! What does she do? She would get to know the price of things if she had to earn, and see how a rupee is made,' father says loudly.

'You brute! All those years I served you diligently. If I had known what would happen to me I would have jumped in a well rather than let them marry me to you,' mother answers with tears spilling all over.

'You can undo the marriage now. Go back to your father and see if he'd support you. If you don't come back within a fortnight, I am not the son of a Brahmin,' father laughs cynically.

'Who says you are? A sweeper would show more charity than you! I'll go away and never see your face again!' Mother's voice is highpitched with anger.

'Shanta, Vijay, mother and father are quarrelling again and mother is sobbing and packing her things. She is going to leave us,' says Asha in panic and despair.

'Mother, please don't cry, when I grow up I will earn lots of money and give it all to you. You are good and kind and father is mean and bad. In fact, he is a devil, I don't like to go near him. And when I grow up I'll chop his head off with a sword,' says Vijay.

'No child, he isn't wicked. It is just my unlucky fate. If only I had learnt how to read and write and had been taught to earn my living I would not have stayed in this helpless position,' mother tells Vijay and Asha.

Tears rain on the pillow like a heavy downpour. Mother's eyes are like wells full with water, and her cheeks are salty. Mother's belly is soft, soft like cottonwool. She smells like the grass and the freshly rained-on earth. To lie with her on the bed is like reaching heaven.

FATHER

All my forefathers were born in this little village and all of them grew up in dirt, married, lived, produced and died. I can see all of them in front of my eyes. There is my father sitting in the winter sun from morning till evening, puffing at his hukkah. The most he ever did was to fill it again with a pinch of tobacco and, of course, when we could do that for him he even stopped doing that. He would get up at 4 am in the summer but just sit in the kitchen and smoke. Why, the man was so lazy that he would not even bathe himself, so your Grandmother had to bring a bucket of water for him at 4 in the morning and just empty it on his head!

No, life has not changed an iota since I was a child. They say the wheel of time moves slowly but here I am sure it does not move at all. I remember his routine when I was a child so well. He sat in the square playing shatranj (chess) till late in the afternoon. Then he went to a farmer to demand some fodder for his cow, paid a hurried visit to the temple and the day was over. This is the normal day for most Brahmins. I bet they do exactly the same now. It makes me wonder how much these people value time. They squat there all day, struggling with Knights and Kings. But damn their Knights, and damn their Kings, and damn their dignity of being high and mighty Brahmins. Why, they are worse off than the Harijans! They would think it below their dignity to do a stroke of work, and in their homes their wives and daughters may carry on living, often half-dressed and half-starved. They provoke my anger so much! No wonder I have nothing to do with them. I tell you, child, if you want to get ahead, keep away from them. They are the vipers, the aimless do-nothings!

They do not know the dignity of labour and hard work, and if they carry on without change before long they will be completely wiped out and their place will be taken by the industrious, by the honest. They are so priggish too. They like to remember the past glory of some 2,000 years ago when their mighty ancestor wrote a Treatise on the *Vedas** – the *Sankhya Darshan*. Why, they can't even read the book, much less understand its erudite truths. God damn them all! It makes me so angry.

When I saw my father wasting his life away, just sitting there day after day, smoking his head off and not even bothering to shake the ants and flies off him, I wondered what he had to live for and truly wished him dead! I saw no purpose to his life. His living was no better than being dead, it was so uneventful. And I am not embarrassed, now, to think that I wished him dead at that time. My views have not changed since; in fact, I am convinced that life means action and nothing more. So, do not waste time children or time will waste you.

Like a group of timid sheep we children roamed and wandered together. We filled our laps with wild convolvulus and dandelions. We made chains of water lilies and hung them round our necks. We paddled in the mud pools and emerged wearing mud socks and shoes and lotus chains. We pretended we were sea nymphs emerging from the foamy ocean. But here in our ocean there was no foam but grey-green weeds and green pond water! No graceful dolphins danced here with their ethereal, curved bodies save the little tadpoles, and instead of the giant sharks we had the pond turtles which looked fierce and sage-like with their long necks exposed. They sat on swaying logs or in the naked roots of some decayed tree in the noonday sun with their eyes closed. We were happy in our haven of dusty, rutted roads and mud houses. Each sunrise was a new beginning and each sunset a new experience, so hungry were we for life. We gathered mushrooms in the green fields strewn with manure, and ate them with relish. Some of them might have been toadstools but we survived. We also tried succulent chickweed and other strange weeds and thrived.

Some children peeped out of a tumbledown house of handmade bricks. Their noses were running on dry, caked lips. They had

* The four *Vedas* are the earliest known religious books. Kapila Muni was the author of a philosophical system known as *Sankhya*.

gummed eyes and uncombed hair. They were the children without any clothes or shoes on, poor-looking and poorly looked after. The house was on the outskirts of the village and our neighbours were from the Harijan quarters.

'Hello, are you our new neighbours?'

(Mouth twisted in scorn – I, a town born and town bred, a civilised being, I shall not speak to these dirty tadpoles.)

'Vijay, come and play with me, come and play houses with me.'

'Vijay, let us go and fly our kites. Vijay, let us come and look into that well.'

'Hello there!' 'Hello, there!' echoing voices answering back with double ferocity out of the deep, dark earth, mocking the self-imposed, class-ridden loneliness.

'This is the Grandmother of the well, that is why she is so deep-voiced. All Grandmothers are!'

'Sing a song about a soldier, Asha, I like soldiers.'

> *Once there was a Soldier*
> *He marched to Lahore*
> *He had a pair of too-big boots*
> *And he fell across the floor!*

'Hurray the Grandmother Well sings it with us. Come on, sing again loud, louder and yet louder till echo follows echo and nothing is left but a gigantic crash, a splash, a tear down, a thunder, a storm, a most horrible, big, booming noise embracing all directions, all-pervading! Rest, O You Spirits of the Well for centuries. Strong, frightening, yet obscure in the dark, still, deep waters.'

'Jitu, are you taking the buffalo for a bath to that big pond in the middle of the fields where the acacias bud down and look at their gold-laden faces? Where the mustard blooms on all sides, and the roads are covered with yellow gold and the sky is blue?'

We go along with Jitu to the pond and as the buffalo steps into the water, we sit on her sleek, soft back as she slides into the pond like a dart. It is exhilarating and enthralling. It is inspiring. A ride on our buffalo's back equals none. Her back is smooth like satin, her skin is warm, polished and shiny and she is gentle like a cow. She is like a big whale swimming out in the deep sea and we her crew! We advance upon a group of children and try to enhance the new-made acquaintances. We are bold and aggressive while the children are shy, and as we speak they break into a titter and run away shouting, 'They speak funny! They come from the city!' And we come home with slouching gaits, our hands thrust deeply in our pockets, like hang-dogs.

The house is big and strange. It has only two rooms and no kitchen. The courtyard is like a field overgrown with foot-high grass and a cluster of trees like a miniature wood. There is a big, old mulberry tree in one corner, with toadstools growing in its exposed roots. The toadstools are so gigantic that not only the toad, but we too, can sit on them comfortably. There is also a shisham tree, with shimmering, round leaves. It was cut down six times but each time it sprung up with double the energy and added height. Father says it has a will to survive, and if a thing has got a will to survive you cannot kill it. Also there is the giant margosa tree whose girth must be at least fifteen or twenty feet. It is inhabited by a colony of crows, sparrows and endless parrots. Apart from these friends, wasps, butterflies, moths and iguanas thrive on it. Its fragrance is supposed to be healthy and expel flies and mosquitoes but they too seem to thrive and flourish here. There are many other saplings and bushes too numerous to mention. In the courtyard there are rows upon rows of stables where our Grandfather kept horses. At the farther end, there is a verandah with yet more stables and two little store rooms for straw and dry hay.

This is going to be our home for ever and ever.

The street it is in has no name since it is still under pasture land in the records. At the mouth of the street there is a blacksmith's one-roomed smithy, then there is a derelict plot of land which has sky-high heaps of waste, manure and cowdung. Sometimes in this tangle of weeds it yields such delicacies as melons, cucumbers, squashes and even tomatoes. Some parts of this plot have been divided into sections by the zealous neighbours, and each has a claim to a certain area and territory. Here they make dung-cakes to stack and dry in the sun till they can be burnt and consumed in the hearth to make chapattis and curries where they smell with a sweet, wood-smoky aroma. You can view here all the artistic skills of the women who spend their time making most elaborate, zig-zag, floral and crescent-shaped patterns with these cakes. There are squares in military precision, oblongs and rounds of cakes. The whole field has the neat look of a well-behaved regiment of a certain ingenious commander who has arranged his unit in such orderly patterns. Here the eye wanders so slowly and soothingly till it reaches a bright yellow spot, a gigantic sunflower in this haven.

Then there is the grand, old, dignified house itself. Standing like a palace in its lone glory. Then, there is another empty box with a door to it. It used to be a house owned by the Muslims but now it is free for anybody's use. Most likely ours! After that there's the lame carpenter's worskshop. The carpenter has bright little eyes, and hair white as snow, and he hops on one leg and a homemade stick and goes joggety jog. The carpenter is friendly and drinks gallons of lassi (buttermilk) with salt, then belches and belches till he is ready to consume another bucket. He just puts his toothless mouth to the bucket and swallows. He is like a little sea-horse with a white beard and a moustache. Then there are some other deserted plots. They were bought very cheaply at a time of the owners' prosperity. But the price of land never went up. So they just stayed there forsaken, alone and deserted. They are now covered with green bush, briar, bamboo, weeds and the giant acacias. Many kinds of thistle grow here. They would supply a rich natural resource to the botanist who will no doubt arrive one day. They provide us with a good, well-concealed, private lavatory. We just creep in there when we need to, and observing nature at close quarters is an added bonus. However, the snakes are there too with their hissing, pink tongues, wriggling, diamond bellies and with mongoose and vultures to keep them company. Then, at the very end of the street, there is another ruined Muslim dwelling, a casualty of partition. In here lives a strange, weird, half-naked man with his herd of goats and obscure men friends who make illicit liquor. These men, we are told, are petty thieves, gamblers and layabouts with creeping ways and sneaky, narrow eyes which seem to observe all, even when purposely pointed to the ground. On the other side of the street there is a one long, bizarre encampment, a mere encirclement of the land, with low foundation walls with doors in them to mark it as a private territory. It was bought by a prosperous carpenter who happened to go to East Africa to reap some of the riches there. However, when he came back he had more money than he knew what to do with. So he bought the whole side of the street and just built walls around, sticking doors and windows in them without building any rooms. On the road end, however, he built a huge room with very high walls which still functions as the religious committee meeting room for the Riat community. On the other side, he felt more inclined to exercise his aesthetic abilities and make some sort of orchard. So he planted two pomegranates, a guava, a lemon and some orange trees. But most of them never reached maturity and the ones that did never bore fruit. So the orchard, like the rest of the territory, stayed an unfinished dream of a man now aged and blind who had seen better days.

The blind end of the street was encircled by a low wall. If you jumped this wall, which was quite easy, you reached a strange territory of ditches and dykes. This was the area where the earth was dug to make bricks when my Grandfather's brick kiln first started. However, after the years when bricks replaced mud houses, this area expanded. These dug-up, quarry-like places serve ideally as the open-air lavatories for the whole of the village. So, from early each morning, newly married, aged, infirm and children pay a visit to this place twice daily. They come in groups like many-hued butterflies in an array of fine clothes sitting close to each other to chatter endlessly while they respond to nature. They are used to this social interaction and do not feel at all shy or embarrassed at showing and exposing their different sized, hued and dimpled buttocks. Some come with children and they sit the child deftly on one knee while they pay homage to nature. They have no conveniences at home and these are the only outside toilets available. These places are never cleaned except by the action of nature which is slow and long. So the wind that blows from that direction to our house is particularly full of life and aroma but we are now used to it and don't mind.

At the other end of the street there is a deep, muddy pond. Most of the waste from half the village pours into it which it accepts with benign indifference. In the summer, the heat putrefies it a little but it is bad in the rainy season when it overflows its banks and starts flowing to our house. On the other side the pits fill up with rain water and effluent and the smell is awful. How we manage to stay healthy is another of nature's mysteries (so says my mother). So this, in short, is our ancestral home and street we live in.

FATHER RECALLS

When I was a young man the village was much smaller. Where the house and workshops are, there used to be maize fields as high as six feet tall. I well remember once, when I came to pay a visit to these fields, I was tempted by the ripe corn. I broke a cob but the crack of the stalk made such a noise that the farmer in the other field heard it and I was caught, shamefacedly, red-handed. I was taken to my father who told the farmer to have a section of his field as compensation. But after the man had left he took his shoe from his left foot and administered a dozen strokes to my bare back. I never forgot that lesson and never stole again in my life.

In those days we used to go to the well with a rope and a bucket every morning. We each had a bath first and then we filled the bucket and brought it home full. That particular morning I was helping your uncle to pull the rope and when the bucket was half way up, he let go of the rope, just like that, without a reason. Of course, the bucket and the rope vanished in the well! I was quite taken aback at this when Saggi (your uncle) turns towards me, slaps my face with full force and vanishes for the day. Still, he has not done badly for himself, considering he never even passed his matriculation and had no formal education. Why, he is a damn sight better off than any of us. He started as a shopkeeper but that did not work out because he was never there when somebody came to buy. I knew he would never sit still, but our father, he thought that he needed a helping hand and set him up with the shop. After the shop failed, he roamed around for a year or two doing odd jobs, smoking, gambling, riding horses and playing shatranj. Then he married and he could not very well do what he wanted. So he learnt some legal language and became a letter writer, setting himself up as an expert in writing deeds and official applications. It worked out very well since the whole farming crowd turned to him. People were all illiterate and Saggi Lala knew just what they wanted him to write. He grew so expert in this that he could compose a letter without asking the person what sort of letter he wanted written. And, oh, the person would be full of admiration for his skill and say, 'Lala, you knew what I wanted, that is just the sort of letter I wanted but I could not figure out how to say it!' Soon Saggi was making more money than anyone else in the village. But he has never left the village, not even for a day. His life has just revolved around it and perhaps he will die one day without seeing anything of the world. Still, financially, he is better off than any of us and knows how to make money. Also he got the lion's share of our father's property, the brick business, the sugar mill and the best of the land. That was another trick they played on me. When father died he left all the farming land in one piece. Part of it was poor soil which depended on rain water and the rest was arable, fertile land with irrigation facilities. Anyway, your uncle said, to determine who should have which portion, we should draw lots and for this he approached your distant uncle Sri Ram who was supposed to be the impartial judge. He was asked to select three sticks, one for each of us, and, naturally, I got the worst lot, nothing grew there except the desert thistles and lizards.

I had to pay tax on the land and buy seed which grew poorly. One of the fields has a hill in the middle and the rain water just drains off to the sides so nothing grows in the middle. You know the field we call 'The Pot Bellied'. Until recently I believed that it was just my luck till a few days ago Sri Ram sent a message for me to go and see him. He was sick and called me to his bedside and said, 'I have thought of unburdening myself to you so many times and admit a wrong that I did to you. I could never face myself admitting my crime. Now I am a dying man and you will forgive me. You know thirty years ago, when I stood drawing lots as an impartial judge, I knew all along which lot to draw for any of you. Saggi and I had discussed it all before and your lot was to be the smallest stick!' So shocked was I that you could have knocked me down with a feather.

It was all so odd that I could not utter a word to the dying man who looked at me with a pale, haggard face and staring, pitiful eyes which looked into mine waiting for me to utter the necessary phrase 'All is forgiven'. I was shaking and sweating and I just walked out without uttering a word! No, your uncle and I are very different. It is strange that we are so unlike yet we are brothers. And yet when he was about to be locked away once when he worked in the bank, I was sad for him and cried.

You know Bhagga Singh, that old man with the snow-white beard and turban? Well, he went to Africa and used to send money to the bank to be put in his account. Gradually, he amassed a small fortune. Saggi, Bishnu and Sharni decided that they should share his fortune. Why should the man be well off when they had been looking after his money for so long? They made a number of withdrawals by forging the man's name. When Bhagga Singh demanded to see his account he was puzzled to see so many withdrawals and the signature was his own! Nothing short of a law suit could have brought any justice. In the end handwriting experts were called and the case was decided in his favour, and your uncle and the other two had to serve jail sentences. But they somehow managed to wriggle out of it and were given bail. Bishnu was the only one who had to spend some considerable time in jail and, I bet, he was the least guilty party – even now the poor man has not lost his nickname of 'jail bird'. I think it is unfair for a man to be reminded of his misdeeds all his life. But it is like this in a small village, people never forget or miss anything scandalous and they still call him 'Bishnu the Jail Bird'. Of course, your uncle is a respectable person and people who remember this incident never mention it to him.

He has not made a bad job of his talent but what still puzzles me is why he should begrudge me my property; after all, he had the use of it for twenty-two years when I was away. I had a job to get possession of the house and this land. He called me to his shop and then proceeded to call me a hundred names and insults before an assembly of men of his own following who grinned and smirked. It still hurts me to recall the episode. He called me a 'fool' who is 'governed by a cluster of women' and 'how utterly disgraceful' that your mother did not use the purdah or cover her face 'and went about in a saree'! I thought it was pointless to say anything, I felt too insulted, and walked away. It is strange that we are brothers and yet so unlike each other. We live in a small village where a handful of other Brahmin families live, and yet we must pass each other and not even say 'Hello' like strangers and enemies. However, that is life, my dearest girl!

After the end of summer Vijay and I had to go to school. We dreaded the new school. It was not the place we knew and loved, it was a strange place, an unknown and formidable enemy. It was a Tuesday when Malika, our elder sister, took us both to be registered and left us there amid the enemy. The school had a history of benevolence. It was built, along with a temple and a pond, by a philanthropist who could not have any male heirs. He visited the Ganges and other sacred places and once, when on such a visit, he had a vision in which he was ordered to build a school, a temple and a pond for the whole of the village then his wishes would be granted. However, when these memorials were near completion he was past having any children. He felt he was cheated by fate. So he ordered the work to be stopped. The pond was left without any boundary wall and steps on the fourth side. The temple never acquired its ornamental walls as proposed in the designs. And the school never got its finishing touches. The windows had no glass or steel bars in them. The walls were never pointed and the lavatories never completed. Of course, nobody ever dreamt of maintenance and repairs and the village Panchayat (Council) never had any funds to support the charitable aims.

The frescoes and murals on the only temple in the village had faded. Some of the dwelling quarters for the priests had fallen into disuse and were full of cracks. The whole exterior of the temple was crumbling. On the walls where the scenes from the *Gita** were depicted, a kind of green fungus had crept in. For example, where

*Indian scriptures.

Lord Krishna confiscates the clothing of the bathing shepherdesses because they were not modest and he wanted to teach them a lesson, only the arm of Krishna with a bundle of clothes was visible, and all that remained of the shepherdesses was an eye here, an ear there, part of a naked breast here, and a thigh there. To comprehend the full mural you had to open and shut your eyes fifty times, and then make out some sort of a coherent mass from jumbled-up limbs by using your imagination.

The pond, of course, had exceeded its boundaries because it was constantly dug down by people to obtain clay to make into bricks. At one time it stood six feet away from the school but now it came up to the front of it. The school had receded back into it and it looked like an island, surrounded by water on three sides. In the rainy season, the water reached the back windows and the girls floated their wooden writing blocks tied on the neck by pieces of string. These blocks were oblong, flat pieces which had handles on them to hold on to, a bit like chopping boards. They were used by the children for calligraphy using reed pens and India ink. They were cleaned daily after school, prepared for writing with a coat of plaster from a block of ochre. Girls used the pond to wash and prepare the boards for the next day, and many a girl got a ducking and nearly drowned but was always rescued by the diligent, watchful eye of the teacher and other girls.

Vijay cried; he did not want to go to the boys school, he wanted to stay with me, so he went to this school. But the girls laughed and I hated them for it. I wanted to run away from the school. I did not like the teacher who had a cruel, piercingly shrill voice and an ugly, pointed, vixen-like face. She also had a malicious, short laugh. She favoured certain children who fetched and carried for her, and disliked others. When I first met her I knew instinctively that we were not going to be friends. I missed old Yashpati, the man who used to pat me kindly and tell me that I was a clever child. The girls were older than me and cruel too. I was lonely and had no friends. I was ordered to sit at the tail-end of the class, just where the hessian mat had run out. So I had no alternative but to squat in the dust. The teacher sat at the top of the class in a chair and shouted sums at me, and by the time the words floated to me, I had ceased to listen or could not hear. So all my sums were wrong and there were crosses all over my slate. With each new cross my agony increased, and I felt humiliated before the whole class. I who used to be always at the top. At the end of the day Vijay and I disappeared as fast as we could and ran home.

Oh, the misery of it all. Each new morning now came as a stranger and the sun was the enemy. I hated the beginning of the day and mourned the end of the day. My mornings were mournful, my evenings full of sorrow, and the days at school passed slowly. Each day an added injury was sustained. The girls bullied me. They bullied my speech, they made fun of my stature, they carried me when I did not wish to be carried, and threw me into the air, my body spreadeagled like a bat's. When I was asked my name I added glamour to it by prefixing an adjective and called myself Madhu Asha. The girls fell about laughing and corrupted the pronunciation so it sounded vulgar and rude. And the teacher was always sitting there like a cruel cat with an odious grin on her face and beady eyes sizing me up. I hated her: if only I could kill her and wring her short neck, take her scheming eyes out and throw them in the murky pond.

I thought of a hundred different tales to tell my mother so that I did not have to go to school. I faked stomachaches, headaches, nausea, fevers and many other ailments but no one gave me a reprieve. I dreaded school. I did not know my tables and I did not know how to divide. The teacher would ask me every day to recite the tables up to twenty times twenty whilst father had always told me that it was not necessary to learn them after tens. In the end I grew desperate and invented an elaborate tale, one that my mother and sisters would really believe.

'Mother, I don't want to go to school. (Floods of tears.) Yesterday, the teacher hit me and the steel bangle got imbedded in my arm. She doesn't like me.'

'Why did she hit you? What did you do?'

'Nothing. She just called me to her desk and hit me!'

29

'Why? Look at your arm, how it is all sore and swollen! How dare she? You wait till your father hears of it, the bitch! The whole village is against us, and I never trusted that woman.'

'May I stay at home, mother? I could do all my sums at home and I could read to you out of the *Gita* when you churn milk each morning like I used to do, when we were happy! (More tears.)

'You are telling me the truth, child? I don't understand, for the life of me, I don't, why should she do a thing like that? Especially if you gave her no cause to be angry. But you can never understand some women,' she said rather thoughtfully. 'I tell you what, I will go myself and take you to the school and tell that teacher to keep her dirty hands off you!'

How unwillingly I dressed that morning! How many more excuses did I think of and reject. How dejected was I at the thought of being found out. 'Mother, don't tell the teacher I told you that she hit me, if you do she might hit me some more.'

'Why? Child, she is not a despot. I will take you right to the headmistress and inform her of the heinous cruelty of that woman.' My feet were like lead as I tottered behind, found excuses to delay my departure and then followed my mother who fussed and grumbled at my extreme slowness. I wished the earth would split open and swallow me forever. I wished I could grow some wings and fly away. But none of these wishes materialised and I, a mere mortal girl, was at the school gates on time. My mother's anger had increased and she was now flaming mad as she pushed me into the headmistress's room and showed her my lacerated and swollen arm and told her of the fine work that was being undertaken in her school by the junior staff, which consisted of nothing but punishing innocent children. I thought of all the pain I had gone through the previous evening with that piece of blunt wire, and how it was hurting now.

The headmistress sent for the teacher. I wanted to run away from the room but was caught and dragged back by my mother. My mother said, 'See for yourself, how frightened she is and how pale the poor child turns even at the mention of the teacher's name.' Anyway, when the teacher came the headmistress briefly told her of the accusation and asked her for an explanation. You should have seen the teacher's face. It was so red and nasty-looking as she glowered at me. And then she bent her shoulders back and gave a short, snorty laugh. She said, 'Have you been up to your old tricks again, Asha? Why, the girl is a plain liar. I never touched her. I swear on the *Guru Granth*.' My mother was furious and screamed, 'How dare you say that of my child? Why, I know my child. She would never tell a lie. She has been brought up in a Brahmin household.'

'Nevertheless it is a lie,' said the teacher and she marched out. My mother yanked me out of the little room despite the headmistress's protestations, and I felt relieved that that would be the last time I would go to school. I was rather pleased that my painful efforts had yielded fruit and I was reprieved.

'Can I come with you, Father?'

'Yes, come on! Bring the other sickle and rope.' Away we go marching on a dusty road, a dusty road full of ants, and a dusty road covered with dried leaves and sugar cane peelings, a dusty road with odd bits of paper fleeing. A thorn pierces my heel, I pause without a wince and very deftly take it out. Put some spit on the sore part and run again on one foot to be with my father again. I can carry all the clover in the world on my shoulders and my head. A great, huge, giant bundle of it, all on my own. O, I am big and strong. The clover smells sweet, it is soft and dark green with pretty pink flowers. As I carry it, it makes a fine lacy curtain in front of my eyes and I run with it on my head so it wobbles and bounces. I find a hollow stem and press it in my palm, put it to my mouth and blow in it. And the sound comes shrill, melodious and sweet. Sometimes the music is fast and broken, sometimes it is piercing and sweet. The fat, fast caterpillars that hide in clover creep in my shirt and tickle me till I jump and they fall to the ground. This little head of mine carries bundles of barley bravely, bundles of clover, of maize, grass and hundreds of other tasty substances that cows can enjoy. Not only can I carry the heavy bundles but I can handle the sickle just as deftly as a farmer's son can, and cut corn, maize, sugar cane, wheat or cotton stalks and reap with a sickle at speed. I can also make a rope of hay or flax and twist it in no time. I can milk a cow or tame a naughty

heifer or a dog in a trice. I only have to whistle and all the creatures
are at my heels. I am better than the Sorcerer's Flute. I can make the
creatures dance as I like without a pipe and do as I wish. I roam the
wild woods and the fields all by myself, and all the freedom of the
wild is mine. The blue convolvulus bends in my fingers and becomes
a dainty, fragrant cup out of which I can lick honey and nectar and
drink the morning dew.

We go hand in hand, my father and I, in the early hours of the
still morning, over the river before the sun rises, and the glory of the
rising sun is ours. All the singing birds with their songs are ours. We
can tell them apart before they have opened their beaks. That one is
the Indian woodpecker. Do you see its buff tail, its straw-like beak
and black markings? See how systematically it goes pecking up the
acacia. That sparrow-like creature in the wheatfields is the Indian
bulbul, a singing bird with a beautiful voice but a dull coat. Have you
heard the sugar cane cock? Doesn't it have a horribly raucous voice?
And that near the pond is the Giant Crane in the rushes. See how it
sits with eyes shut, on one leg. There is a story that the crane
imitates a holy man indulging diligently in prayer in the early
morning. The fishes are fooled by this attitude. They take him as
their friend and creep beside him and he swallows them whole.
That is where the saying 'as holy as a crane' comes from. This, here,
is the whole family of sugar cane cocks, here is a toad, and there over
yonder is a brown mongoose. The sun comes up over the sand piles
and shines over the low fields. All the morning songs begin here.
All the shadows are born here too. They are long and thin beneath
the acacias, fat and short under the peepul and the banyan. The
leaves of the peepul and the banyan twist and dance in the sun like a
song, a song that is sung with a wonderfully sweet melody without
words. A song that has a hundred compositions and still many left.
A song that keeps adding to itself forever under the sun, in the long,
sandy stretches of fields amid the sand dunes where the lizards hop
and the field mice breed freely, where sometimes everything that is
green is wiped out by the locusts who sweep the horizons like dark
clouds. After they have gone, there is nothing but desolation and
devastation. After their departure the sand dunes are sieved with
holes and their eggs, which look like barley ears, are dug deep into

the dunes. Out of these pop black, hopping, ant-like creatures which, on reaching maturity, become locusts and begin the cycle all over again. The sun here rises blood red and soon in a moment becomes a burning orb which shines on the dunes and makes them burning hot, so hot that if you walk barefoot at three or four in the afternoon your feet would get blistered in ten minutes. You would die of thirst and exhaustion.

'Are you at home, Malika's mother? I only came to borrow a few seers of flour. We seem to be short of it. By the way, did you hear about Mindi – the granddaughter of Teja Singh?'

'No, I don't think I have. Why? Isn't everything all right with them?'

'Far from it. Mindi died in hospital yesterday. I told you she was a bad one. She would go in for men. She liked their company and see what has come out of it! She was expecting they say. Of course, you can imagine the poor mother's plight. She had to do something about it to save the family's Izzat. So she went to this elder and got a rupee's worth of opium and she gave it to the girl in her porridge. I could feel sorry for the girl because she was young and pretty, then you understand the mother did not have any choice except to end her life and save the family's Izzat! God knows, what has come over girls nowadays. When we were young we did not even let a man's shadow fall over us. It is so sinful and filthy. They took her to the hospital but it was too late. She bled to death. The police were informed and the constables came, and they were going to take her away for post-mortem but the grandfather intervened. He stopped the constables advancing and pointing to his snow-white beard he said, "See my age," and he took his turban off and put it at their feet and said, "My Izzat is in your hands." Then some elders came and begged them to understand the family's shame. Of course, the police understand. Anyway, they all made plenty of money out of it!'

'My goodness,' said mother, 'I did not know a thing about it. That's why I always say that people with daughters should never forget God and always be on the alert. It is bad to have a daughter who doesn't think of her parents' Izzat. Why, such daughters should always be strangled in infancy. But you can never tell what they are going to be when they grow up. I always pray to God that if any of mine are going to be like Mindi then kill them now, strike them dead, and take them off now when they are still innocent and the family is unblemished.'

'It is different with your girls, you always teach them such good manners.'

'Why, if I had had half a chance and had been educated I would never have got married! Not that I have got anything to complain about, you understand. Malika's father has always been faithful. Though he is quick-tempered he does not mean any harm!'

'Yes,' said the neighbour, 'I do know his nature. Last time when I came to borrow a bucket he showed me to the door. I had to laugh, I knew he didn't mean it!'

'It is Iron Age though, as I was saying to Dhanno the other day about Channo's niece. The girl is as gentle as a lamb and butter wouldn't melt in her mouth. She never met a man's eye and kept hers always downcast to the ground. And the grand marriage they made of her only a year ago. The jewellery and the clothes, everything was so nice! I hear now that they are fighting a law suit in the courts. It was the father-in-law: the son was a bit simple and the old man wanted to sleep with her! He got hold of her in the kitchen while the mother-in-law was out in the fields! She put up a struggle and he beat her, the poor girl! She had a very bad time and in the end she gave up and told her mother what she was going through. Oh my Rama, Rama! You know how quick-tempered her mother iṣ, she went straight to their house and told the man what she thought of him. Right in front of the son. "But if this is the way things are in your family, why, I would just like my husband to get on top of your daughter", she said. And, "I married her off not to sleep with you but with your son!"'

The women called upon the names of various gods and goddesses to save them, held their earlobes in a most awed, repentant manner, and yet chuckled at the remarks and adjusted their duppattas (scarfs), suddenly becoming over aware of modesty. Then the other adjusted her round-framed glasses, tucking the wires behind her ears. She was just about to launch into another piece of gossip when she heard a man's footsteps, she just tucked the bag of flour under her arm, adjusted her duppatta again, rushed towards the door and was gone!

'Was that old bag of a woman here again?' Raju demanded. 'I will have to break her legs to stop her! Why, the nerve of that God damn, gas bag of a woman! Why, the nasty rumourmonger! I bet she can't digest her food until she has been around a few houses and opened her dirty bag of stories! The old, hook-nosed, bitch-assed, God damned bag of a bitch.'

'Be quiet, calm down, Malika's father. She is not so bad and I didn't give her anything. She was only talking to me. I haven't got many people to talk to around here and you would stop her coming too? That was always your aim. To take me to a desert and leave me to die of loneliness. You can't bear anyone talking to me, not even that poor woman. I know you are jealous of her. You are wicked through and through.' (Sobs and tears.)

Then there ensued another battle. The man, bitter and full of hatred for the small-time village mentality, and indignant at not being understood. The woman, tear-soaked and sullen, biting her lips and wiping her eyes again while the smoke from the kitchen rose gently towards the sky in ringlets and curls, and the utensils made a terrible din, bang and clatter! The anger of the mother sought expression in the beating of the saucepans, clatter of the lesser objects and all the time Asha lay hidden underneath the charpoy learning about Izzat.

The house was gradually emerging from the rambling stables. All the trees were down except the giant margosa. The walls were fairly high now. There was a kitchen and a bathroom in the house. It had a very spacious brick courtyard with mosaic flooring. There was also a large verandah with round columns. Proper staircases were being built to link the top floor and some rooms were being added to, to make it into a two storey Kothi. Though the house had never been planned it seemed to have a certain uniformity; it appeared to be better than any other houses owned by the well-off people in the village.

As the house was on the outskirts of the village, its back joined on to the houses owned by the Harijan people. And from the stair steps one could see Harijan women and children squatting in rows in the early morning sun preening each other's hair, combing and rubbing oil into it. Originally, the properties belonged to people who had left for Pakistan, and some of the residents were Hindu refugees from Pakistan. The history of these houses was a closed book to all of them. As they had not built them or played any part in their planning, most inhabitants paid little attention to the environment or the facilities.

These houses had no drainage system in them nor any proper means of lighting. They were just one- or two-roomed little mud huts with thatched roofs. Most of the people provided cheap labour for the landowners and farmers who never paid them in cash. They were grossly exploited by every race. Some were skilled weavers, others leather workers, shoemakers and butchers. They all lived in a closely related community and were intermarried. The light of reform had not reached the village yet, so they were still called by their derogatory caste names, but they did not resent this. Of course, the mere change of name into Harijan would not have helped them at all. They would still have been poor, their women exploited, ill-fed and ill-clothed. They were not allowed in houses, nor in kitchens, nor did they ever wish to enter. We had reserved utensils for them which were kept in an alcove in the entrance, and after a full day's work they were given a few chapattis to eat as part of their wage. Their women could not afford to have any dignity or Izzat and many farmers raped them or sexually exploited them for a few items of clothing and a good meal. Quite a few of their children were fathered by the farmers and the men from the Harijan area were resigned to it. They appeared to have no control over their destiny. They often shared their cramped quarters with cows and buffaloes and chickens, and had poor ventilation. The children got government scholarships and free books if they wished to study but, sadly, not one girl was sent to school and they all stayed illiterate. Asha would spend some time with one or two of the girls and try to teach them the primer but this could only be done away from her mother's and grandmother's eyes as they forbade her to have any contact with them. Evidently, the children could not spend their scholarship money on anything but books and parents could not afford to lose their labour as they always wanted extra hands for menial jobs and field work. Their children started working from the age of three. A girl of three looked after the youngest child, went gathering sticks and cowdung on the dirt roads and, if she had some spare time, her mother gave her a sickle and a bag so that she could go to the footpaths and cut wild grass and greenery for the goat, or if they had no goat then enough to sell to buy salt for the day. Girls and women obviously bore the brunt of this stark life, carrying the heaviest burdens. Some of their offspring were married at a very young age, sometimes as young as eight or ten. Out of a housing area of a hundred or so, only one boy went to school and his name was Darshan. His mother proudly maintained that she was not like others but different. She was a tall, thin, dignified widow, and he was her only son, and she was known simply as Darshan's mother. Women seemed to be only known by their relationship to males, either as mothers, wives or sisters.

The boy had a faultless manner and a very immaculate dress sense. He dressed in dazzling white and always had his hair neatly parted in the middle. He was not well liked by the lesser Harijan brothers for his airs and graces and they thought he was going beyond his poor mother's means. They complained that his mother did hard labour for him; she had gone grey and her knuckles had turned white keeping his clothes spotless in a dusty mud hut. Indeed there were stories that when Darshan went to the open-air lavatory and squatted in the cotton fields, he was seen to take a mirror out of his pocket and start combing his hair!

Anyhow, when Darshan failed to qualify for the school leaving certificate for three consecutive years, his mother lost heart or maybe the resources ran dry. But Darshan could not give up his hard-earned dress sense and polished shoes. To make him conform his mother arranged his marriage, and he had a son.

However, he was not fitted for an ordinary Harijan's life after having gone to school! So his mother borrowed fifty rupees and set him up in a shop in the Bazaar, but people just ignored him and did not buy anything from his shop. Perhaps they thought it was below their dignity to buy from a Harijan. Nor did they like the idea of a Harijan moving into the merchant class. So they just went past his shop and bought from the next one.

After wasting six months he moved to the Harijan colony where everyone welcomed him and fawned over him. He was busy every day till midnight and got up early in the morning. His trade seemingly flourished but sadly his income decreased, and within another six months he had to pack up and come back to the old Bazaar where obviously his trade did not flourish but he could always be assured that his shelves would be full.

The thing that went wrong amid the Harijans was, of course, that they never had any cash and Darshan let them have groceries on credit, but when the time came to pay up they accused him of being mean to his own folk. So poor Darshan's shop is still there in the Baazar as a symbol of high aspirations in caste struggle, and he sits there idly swatting the flies and smoking. If, occasionally, he finds another idler like himself, they start playing cards so this passes his day.

In the long moonlit nights I lay still and listened to the cries of the night. It was the time when one saw ghosts and spirits of skeleton trees and the odd human being prowling. They were creatures of the night who came out like spiders at dusk, wove their webs and disappeared. Such a one was our neighbour, a big, hefty woman with huge, bushbaby eyes, a thin, cadaverous face and sticking out teeth. We were told never to peep through her windows or spy on her but this made us even more curious and eager to do so. Suddenly the woman assumed a disproportionate fascination for me. She was married twice already when she came and occupied the other side of the street. As soon as she came she tried to exert her authority over the old man (her husband) and her husband's mother. The father-in-law, an ancient, white-bearded figure, had worked hard to acquire all the property for his only son and had now arrived back from Kenya almost blind. The old lady was a quiet, unassuming person. She was also short-sighted but not completely blind. Her face was lemon-wrinkled and sallow, she rarely laughed but seemed to live in perpetual fear of offending her daughter-in-law. Soon the daughter-in-law acquired all the keys to the different parts of the house and gave the mother and father-in-law a little cell room to live in. They were not allowed in the kitchen any more but some dry bread and lentils were taken to them twice daily. Strangely enough their son never questioned any action she took and always kept quiet. So much so that the old lady was convinced that he was under some spell or charm acquired by the daughter-in-law. Jito (the daughter-in-law) had no children until, after four years of marriage, she produced a son. He was a strange-looking child who resembled a piglet rather than a human baby and was always devoid of any expression. He also developed a coarse and tormenting nature. When he was about two he displayed a remarkable amount of cruelty. He would take a stick and strike his grandma and grandfather while the mother generally laughed at his antics. He also knew most swear words. It was said that the first word he uttered when he could talk was to call his mother a 'bitch'. Anyway, it was rumoured that his nature was of his uncle's, whose true child he was, rather than his father's. Women's reputations soon sank low in these parts and when Jito had a daughter it was rumoured that she belonged to a holy man the mother frequented. There were tell-tale signs that she was his, as he often came to the house with his followers, and is said to have bragged publicly that 'Goody' was a present to the woman for all the care she showed him.

But nobody dared say anything openly to Jito. She was quick to pick quarrels and always had numerous battles going on. She would fabricate some awful stories about the party in question and soon shut them up with colourful yarns about the woman's morals which made the contestant squirm, feel embarrassed and disappear from the battlefield. She was never friendly with women but a large number of men got on well with her. She was only aggressive with people of her own sex and generally rebuffed any offers of friendship from women. But when talking to a man she would become strangely mellow, her gruff voice would suddenly take on a sweet, husky tone, her eyes would sparkle, smile mysteriously and her body rocked from side to side in a most voluptuous fashion.

During the summer months she took most of her clothes off and roamed around in pants and a bra. She was proud of her long, well-made legs and took a great deal of care and time polishing them with mustard oil. However, she had a very ill-proportioned bust. One of her breasts was exceedingly large like a fat juicy melon and the other was the size of a small orange. She used to put wads of cottonwool in the hollow of the other cup to make it the same size. She also exerted an influence through windows. She only had to go near one and all the layabouts somehow got the scent and swarmed outside her window to whistle, wink, steal a kiss or slap her buttocks. We found these antics fascinating. It was at night though that she came to life. She would dye her grey hair, put mascara in her eyes and brighten her teeth with a special nut, and wear bright lipstick. Then she would put on a black velvet suit, studded with sequins, and an orange duppatta covered with tinsel. Her clothes twinkled in keeping with the night. She had a strange fascination for me, even though I was warned by my mother to keep away from her, and that she was wicked and low. So I stole to her whenever I could and tried her make-up on. She smelt of strong perfumes but at the same time her body had a spicy odour to it. It was a strange kind of smell very peculiar to her person and I wondered if the musk in the deer's navel smelt similar! It reminded me of very ripe pears mixed with cloves.

I was told that at night Jito and her friends roamed around the still night and took over unoccupied houses where they could practise their trade, but I never knew what this was and spent many hours lying awake at night wondering what it could be. Her dress twinkled and her bare feet crept slowly among the tall, thin, dark shadows of houses in the moonlight, gliding away as if on ice and then became one with darkness. A night watchman howled like a dog, knocked on doors and shouted incoherently 'keep awake, and be on guard for burglars'. The village had its thieves and robbers and though people knew who they were, they could never poinpoint them, so petty larcenies and cat burglaries were always going on. There were many burglars and thieves.

The most notorious of the village robbers were the Dakoo brothers. (Dakoo stands for a dacoit or a robber.) There were three of them: Saad, Jis and Jano. It was Saad who was the leader of the gang. They were farmers by profession but found the farm inadequate as they never did any digging or sowing. They were all 'good for nothing', people said, who wanted easy money, except for Jis who did a certain amount of hard work. People said a snake would produce snakes and their father had quite a criminal history himself. In his youth he was accused of homicide and sentenced to death. They say it was his cousin he murdered. He crept to him while he was sleeping and split his skull open with an axe. They say it was a dispute over the land. This cousin of his had a share in the land owned by Saad's father but was not married. Then one day he got into his head that his brother was going to get married and nobody would be able to stop him. So the only possible and logical way was to finish him off. The father, by his sacrifice, gave a substantial start to his children in their life. But as soon as he died they started a still, making illicit liquor and drinking it. They went completely wild, gambled and lost most of the land. They were all married to identical looking, thin, tall, gaunt and ancient looking women, who came from the same village a mile away and accepted their husband's dubious life-style. In fact they were very able hoarders of loot. When the men did a job no one could recover a thing since the three of them travelled overnight and deposited the booty in their parental homes.

Suddenly, one night, everyone was awakened by cries and howls. A woman cried, 'A thief, a robber just behind that far wall! Now what do you want from us poor people?' Soon an army of people appeared, marching with sticks and lanterns; they were all men. They circled, searched and combed every street but they could not find a burglar. It was one of the Dakoo women who had cried and shouted, so people chuckled to themselves that it was a queer joke since who would rob the robbers?

The next day, early in the morning, Pandit Gardhi Lal went to his till and found it bare. He went to the safe – the door was hanging by one hinge and there was nothing in it. He went to the kitchen and found that it was all clean and bare. All his brass pots had gone; he looked for the keys and they were missing. He woke his wife up and she just fainted to see the havoc in the sitting room where everything lay torn in shreds and all the accounts charred. It was obvious that the Dakoo wives had done their job admirably. They had managed to hoodwink the whole village. People knew who cleaned out Pandit Gardhi Lal. The police put the Dakoo brothers in prison but nothing ever came of it. They did not recover a single object and the Dakoo brothers came back proud and victorious, all sleek and fattened up, looking dandier than ever. They put on airs and chased the village girls, even indecently exposing themselves, so the poor girls screamed and ran home. The people in the village were full of terror concerning the brothers and no one dared to leave their homes at nightfall except Jito who was, of course, almost one of them, and laughed away the advances of the Dakoo brothers and whatever they showed off to her.

Early one autumn morning Malika decided to do an act of charity. She was a very good judge of clothes, and one of her friends was getting married, and this friend asked Malika if she could accompany her to the city and choose the materials for her. Now our father never let his daughter travel alone to the city. He was going to the Treasury that day and suggested that Malika and her friend accompany him. So they made packed lunches of stuffed parathas wrapped in a towel, and pickles, then set off to make a day of it. The railway station was three miles away and the quickest way was to walk. Of course, no means of transport were provided by the local council. The road was unmade. It was like a desert road, very sandy and high-ridged, one side of it perpetually piled up with sand and the other side having a deep indentation. The footpath on which people walked single file was more like a tunnel in this uneven landscape. Every summer the storms made the sand piles higher and eroded some more earth, making the footpath deeper. The journey was exhausting since people had to make a constant effort to drag their feet out of the soft sand. The road was only fit for a camel and there were not many camels in the village, so they always trod wearily on foot. Some kind, foresighted person had had a well dug and some trees planted halfway along the journey. Here the footpath rose sharply and the well rested on a raised platform so that the sand could not fill it up. People were ready to take a rest when they reached this spot, and sat down to rest their weary legs awhile and drink the sweet, cool water from the well, and after a rest they were fit to go on their way again. After a few yards the footpath sank once again as the road fell sharply; here another road joined it and made it into crossroads. This was the famous crossroad where people met from different villages and exchanged greetings. This junction, because it was hidden, had a notorious reputation for robberies. It was said that the robbers hid behind the trees watching the roads from a vantage point and when they saw a lone traveller, they jumped on him unawares to take whatever he had on his person. So people always quickened their pace and hurried away from this spot. They hastened their footsteps and almost broke into a trot till they came out of the deep footpath again.

When Malika, her friend and her father reached this crossroads the sun was already hot. So they sat down, ate the stuffed parathas they had brought from home, drank the sweet water of the well and set off again. Malika's father was in such a happy mood that he sang a song in praise of Rama. It was like a nasal chant and he chanted it louder with each step. They reached the railway station in time for the 11 o'clock and Malika's father sat down and relaxed on a wooden seat, took a paper from his crumpled trouser pocket and started reading it. This was a one-line station. There was a station master's office but he had been in the area for so long that nobody queued for tickets. They just wandered in at leisure, had a chat, got the tickets in a leisurely fashion and came out swaggering. The station master also had a way of making trains late. He would not show the green flag until all his friends were on the train. Indeed it was rumoured that the engine driver had got so fed up with being an hour or so late that he had hit the station master with a lump of coal, which was why he still had the nasty gash of a scar on his temple. Nevertheless he still wielded his authority and only gave the signal when he was well and truly ready. This day, too, the train was late; it reached the city late and Raju was a bit short-tempered. When he reached the Treasury there was a mile-long queue and he knew that he would never be able to travel back by the seven o'clock train. Here again the people who knew the treasurer and his staff went through the back door and got paid while the others were kept standing in the burning heat. But Malika and her friend had a good day. They bargained well and now both were loaded with sacks of jari (gold cloth) and velvet. They waited for Raju on the platform but he did not appear till 8 pm when he was tired and short-tempered. However, after resting for half an hour with an iced drink, he felt much better. He grumbled a bit about the unfair attitudes and the inadequacy of the clerks at the Treasury. But gradually he grew calmer and became jovial. He joked about the girl's imminent wedding till she blushed. Then the train came at nine and they boarded it. When they reached the station at the other end it was already pitch dark, and there were no other passengers getting off the train. So they lost no time starting homewards at a brisk pace, chatting, laughing and joking. When they reached the crossroads they could see some black shadows in the distance and Raju asked Malika, 'What are those people doing over there?' Malika replied that there was nothing to worry about – one of the men was obviously urinating and the others were waiting for him. So they carried on walking without a care. But when they reached the crossroads, someone shouted, 'Halt! Don't move an inch.' Poor Raju's wits had left him for the time being. He had never come across a crisis of this magnitude. So he stopped in his tracks and stood rooted to the ground. Two more people stepped out of the dark, their faces masked, and spoke in exaggerated accents. One of them had a gun and this was now poked in Raju's chest and someone shouted, 'If you move or make a noise, we shoot you dead, understand.' And another said, 'We are communists. We are not interested in robbing but we have to inspect everything you have on our leader's orders. Did you see anyone behind you?' The truthful Raju shook his head. By now the moon was up and they could make out a figure sitting in the distance; it was not difficult to guess who he was. It was, of course, Saad. Malika was fond of wearing a lot of jewellery. Soon they had everything stripped off her. She was slow to take her rings off. The man with the gun shouted, 'If you don't hurry, I'll cut your fingers off.' And Raju handed all the money over. They collected all the material they had bought for the wedding and started walking away in an unhurried fashion. The father, daughter and friend still waited, hoping that everything would be given to them after the inspection. After waiting a while they heard a man shout,

'Move, run away or get shot.' So they ran home in a turmoil. Soon everyone in the village was talking about the robbery. The district newspapers carried big headlines, 'Poor Master Gets Robbed', etc.

The robbery was just the beginning. After it poor Raju had to foot the bill for twenty constables and four inspectors who were carrying out the investigation. They stayed for a fortnight and he was poorer than ever. That was the biggest and the most daring robbery that Saad ever pulled. He was put in prison and beaten most severely and starved but they did not recover a penny or get a confession. On circumstantial evidence he was convicted and served a long sentence but after this final sentence he was a changed man. He started taking opium and stopped robbing. One night when he was drowsy after a large dose of opium the brothers just pushed him off the roof. He broke his neck and died. The youngest had his leg broken in a brawl. Gradually their activities came to a halt. Then one morning their old mother was found floating in the pond. She was a thin little woman who came to Malika's house frequently to get drops in her eyes. She always moaned in a pitiful way about how unfortunate she and her sons were; she wiped her eyes with the duppatta and tears rolled down her wrinkled cheeks as she told and retold the cruelties of the police towards her sons and the family.

Her daughters-in-law said that she went to the fields early in the morning and perhaps she was washing herself when she slipped in the pond. People knew better than that. But it was a shock for Asha and Vijay. They had gone out to play and thought perhaps there was a pumpkin in the pond and prodded it with a stick. But when they saw that it was the swollen, naked stomach of a human being they yelled and ran back in fear to their home. It was awful to see a sight like that. The face was all eaten away by fish. There were no nose or eyes. The feet were turned in towards the stomach and they had no toes on them, and both the woman's breasts were eaten up, torn and mauled. They could never forget the sight of that carcass and it even haunted them in their sleep so that they would suddenly cry and yell, 'There's a body, there's a body. Over there in the pond!' And after the accident they could never go to the pond or look at it without seeing more bodies in it!

Of course, no one was hanged for the murder. But sadly it was the finish for the Dakoo brothers too. And an era in the history of Sarē Marē had finally come to an end.

As Asha grew older her awareness and observation of life around her became sharper. She felt acutely the futility of existence for many street urchins.

Lean, scrawny bodies running without clothes on. Their shoeless feet had bleeding toes with bleeding scabs on them. Every time they ran they stubbed their toes again. There was a big 'ouch' and all was forgotten soon. They covered their bleeding toes with pinches of fine dust and the blood congealed. But it was very sore when the scab came off again which it generally did after being knocked by one of the many projecting stones in the street. Their hunger increased with their growing thinness and they wanted more nourishment. It seemed as if they had the capacity to eat all the food in the world. Their hunger was limitless, their lives still unfocused and they yearned for excitement and adventure. But in the quiet farming communities there was nothing exciting except for the mating stray dogs, so they followed them in the day and watched them in the moonlight. They watched with a curious hunger the fight that ensued among a pack of dogs over a bitch. They saw them tear each other apart with fur flying all around. The docile dogs turned into fierce hyenas with burning eyes and bloody faces. They bit, maddened, jostling and pushing to have a go at the bitch. The bitch stayed calm and watched with the passivity of an onlooker whose knowledge is profound and who does not notice the surrounding ignorance.

Some rough boys, who had nothing better to do, ran chasing the dogs, shouting obscenities. They threw bricks, sticks and other weapons at the mating pair and at the fleeing, furious pack. These good for nothing boys climbed the thorny acacias and stole all the eggs from the nesting cranes. They clubbed many a young puppy and kitten to death and watched it writhe in pain. Others they held under water, until the water gurgled in their hollow

47

bellies and the whimpering stopped. They beheaded some cats and cut others' tails off. They watched all this with a certain sadistic pleasure, for they had power over these little creatures.

These were the children of the village.

The boys always marched in groups singing film songs, while the girls sat in groups, spun, told and retold rumours and illicit love affairs and liaisons, and who was consorting with whom. And when they were quiet they imagined themselves to be the heroines of some great romance and free to rid themselves of some of the restrictions that were so much a part of their lives.

There were strong caste barriers. Malika and her sisters were not allowed to mix with these boys. These barriers were further augmented with class barriers, and there were no dealings between them and the other illiterate Brahmin girls. They were seen as snobs and loathed by most of them. They were not allowed to go to fairs or festivals, dances or weddings so the village girls were curious about their sexuality and deeply interested in rumour-mongering.

The other girls were denied all contact with boys, so their curiosity turned towards each other: girls would caress each other, take their clothes off in group bathings and play with each other's breasts in fun, and sit on each other's knees, wrestle and kiss. They compensated for their lack of experience and contact with boys through sexual experiences between themselves which were perfectly acceptable to their families. Asha was always curious about these group explorations and would often go and watch if not participate herself. She was still young and found the growth of breasts and pubic hair an interesting phenomenon. Then one day the girls pulled her down and took her pants off, and crudely told her where babies came from and what men did to women. Her sensibilities were shocked as she ran away home crying, to tell her sister Malika, who forbade her any future contact with the village girls.

Although the expression of sexuality was limited only to their own sex among the village girls, there were cases, sometimes, when a girl overstepped the bounds of propriety and formed an association with a male. That unfortunate girl became such a target of hostility and gossip for the young complacent marrieds and conforming unmarrieds that she sometimes took the extreme step of killing herself or running away. In either case the gossip gave an excitement and vicarious pleasure missing from the girls' lives. These stories were elaborated, embroidered, exaggerated, savoured and relished, and thoroughly indulged and enjoyed. The girls never told these stories in front of men who were the guardians of morality, and who kept control over them through the older, married women. The girls did not gossip in front of older women either.

Malika, because of her aloofness, education and her dress sense, and for not mixing with the village girls, was a target for such malicious stories. She looked down upon the village girls and their preoccupations, and they were out to seek revenge. She put on superior airs, just because she was educated and could write. She associated with men. Men are sexual beings so she must write love letters to them and receive invitations for assignations. So the speculation became a reality, and fantasies turned into actions. Lack of contact and communication with her turned into deep-rooted hostility. When she passed, the girls sniggered, with knowing, leering smiles on their faces. They chanted the names of boys who visited the house under their breaths, and suggested that she was fucking all of them. They made up songs about her loss of virginity, and rumours about her loss of Izzat began to abound. A price had to be paid for her nonconformity. Stories spread to the neighbouring villages. People pointed her out on the buses and in the highways and byways. If she bought an umbrella to shield herself from the rain she was being brazen, and if she wore sunglasses she was seen as thoroughly immoral. If some women stood in a group chatting and she passed by them, cold, mocking eyes followed her. They said it was the mother's fault and the father's stupidity. They lived off her immoral earnings. While all the time poor Malika sat indoors swotting for her exams and learning music. But both these activities were strictly taboo and unheard of, particularly for women. To them she was past marriageable age. The boys they saw flocking to the house came to be coached by her father to gain good marks.

So many notorious stories sprang around Malika that she became a heroine with a pretty bad reputation. The village watched her every move and a thousand eyes followed her wherever she went, such was the nature of local social sanctions and mores. Sometimes stories and rumours abounded about her supposed pregnancy. 'She gave birth to a son in a sugar cane field!', and stories about there being a police enquiry about the death of an infant, and how the police were bribed to keep their mouth shut. Each month the fertile village minds gave birth to a new story when the persecution became too much to cope with. Needless to say Malika was attempting to change this society; she was not a stoic, she broke down and wept many times. She fainted and she grew very, very still. She was a misfit in the village without friends and without confidantes. She seemed proud and haughty and would not converse with anyone. She was an enigma to be attacked and destroyed.

When she was not married off hurriedly people wondered even more; their tactics were not paying off. She was a threat to the status quo and to fathers with unmarried daughters who might copy her. Her father, however, took no notice of what was happening around him. People fell to speculating even more. Malika got a tailor in to get some new clothes made. Stories went around that she was already married and that she had contracted a hurried marriage in a court without her family being consulted. These stories eventually reached Raju's deaf ears via his wife, and his patience was exhausted. These vicious rumours affected Jaya more as she lost the few friends she had made. Every other day people said something to Jaya about her daughter, and she would lash out in a wild fury of rage and tears, and when she came home she lay down, dizzy, sick and exhausted. One day she came in with her breasts and thighs all bruised. The rush of angry hysteria had made her lose control over herself and she had beaten herself with great anger.

The family's stand not to marry their daughter was construed by the elders as defiance of traditional values, and this united the village in their severe condemnation of the family. The display of anger was seen as an added challenge and fuelled the criticism. So much so that the children could not go to school because other children taunted them and said insulting and degrading things to them about their sister. Many times they returned home crying and Malika had to go to the school and confront the children with their lies and made-up tales about her morals.

The ancestral village they had come to for friendship and love now became their enemy. The village elders wished to take away the girl's freedom, thinking that the Raju family were sowing the seeds of corruption and moral decay and undermining their own authority concerning the sanctity of marriage. So they took the necessary steps to make Raju change his stand. They boycotted Raju and his family. He was no longer invited to birth, death and marriage ceremonies by the Biraderi (extended family). That was the ultimate sanction to bring back the wrong-doer to the fold. They had a meeting and outlawed him until he agreed to marry his daughter off. But despite all these pressures, social sanctions and stigmatisation, Raju refused to budge. He was not going to pay a vagabond to keep his daughter; if she had the ability to do other things, she could choose for herself. He wished to do away with dowries and arranged marriages. He further disturbed their peace of mind by stating that his duty was to give Malika a good education suited to her abilities.

Such views were not easy for the people. To them it was a sacrilege, a rebellion against natural laws, so they decided that it was their duty to stop this nonsense. They started working on Jaya by pressurising her, thinking that it was easier to influence and control a woman.

'We married our Janaki yesterday, your Malika is four years older than her. It must be a burden for you. When are you going to marry her off?'

'Whenever she wishes to be married,' said Jaya. Then people started reasoning that there must be something wrong, that they must have something to gain by not marrying her. So the stories were woven and myths were created, and they all caught on like wild woodland fire which spread, raged and crackled, the flames and the smoke spreading in all directions.

In a terrible rage Raju assaulted the local tailor who sewed stories of Malika's marriage out of the clothes he was asked to make. His teeth were knocked out as he wobbled up and down in Raju's grip. He shook like a vine and begged Raju to spare his life and let him go. His whimperings and pleadings were not a pretty sight to see. But when he escaped he went straight to the elders with his tale of being beaten up; the elders were incensed.

'How dare he attack the village and its reputation,' said Raju's own brother, Saggi.

They paid the man to take out a summons for assault. Saggi headed the opposition: he filled in the warrant for his brother's arrest, for defying the might of the village and not appearing before the village Panchayat to answer the charges. The Brahmins and the landowner Sikhs were united in opposition. They wished to curb Raju's rebellion in case other fathers too should start educating their daughters and not marry them according to the age-old traditions of the village. But none of these pressures affected Raju. They speculated that he must have friends in high places who protected him – perhaps he bribed them with the honour of his daughters – otherwise how could a mere schoolmaster bring shame upon the village elders, defy their ancient laws and literally 'set fire to their snow-white beards'? Eventually a summons was sent for his arrest but his good barrister friend from the city intervened and it was withdrawn.

People were still speculating and there was a brief respite in the rumour-mongering but Malika got tired of all this talk. The fire went out of her, so she agreed to settle for a marriage. Jaya breathed a sigh of relief as she had been keen for a long time to give in and celebrate the marriage of her eldest daughter with all due pomp and ceremony. But because Malika was educated, an educated boy had to be found, and all the educated boys Raju saw wanted a prohibitive dowry.

Malika was shown a young man's photograph. He looked handsome and gentle. Malika nearly said 'yes' until she was told that he wanted 40,000 rupees to help marry off his sister and because his parents had spent so much money educating him. Raju still liked the boy and considered ways and means of raising the necessary sum. He maintained that the boy was gentle, and that there were tears in his eyes when he mentioned money, and that it was the custom, the system, that was making people greedy. Raju decided to sell some of his land but Malika would not have any of it. She spat at the photograph, tore it up into little shreds and then threw it on the fire.

OUR FATHER EDUCATES US THROUGH STORIES

In the stillness of the night a story is unfolded which Vijay and I listen to with rapt attention. Our father can tell the best stories and they are all true.

'How many times do I tell you to value time? When you grow up into young men and women, you will remember what your father used to say. Time is precious, time is money, no, time is much more than money, time is LIFE. Now this is the story of Tota Ram which illustrates the phenomenon of time for this village. You all know him, that bald-headed fellow with sticky, red eyes. He goes about without a shirt and his Brahmin's sacred thread displayed on his left shoulder. He is the only man in this village who knows the value of time.'

'Tota Ram, Tota Ram does nothing. He prowls the streets all day long like a stray dog.'

'It is because you can't see him as I see him. It is because you cannot understand the little man that lives inside Tota Ram and only comes out to strike the hour.'

'Tota Ram is foolish, Tota Ram is mad. To see Tota Ram like this, I get very sad.'

'Stop rhyming and listen Asha. You will remember this story for the rest of your life. I knew Tota Ram when I was a boy. He was a brilliant scholar. When it came to school leaving certificate exams he wrote a brilliant essay entitled, "How to make the British leave India in Thirty Days". It was such a clever piece of work, and the State Government became so alarmed, that they refused him permission to go to a State University. He was not allowed to pursue his studies even in the village. In this way poor Tota Ram's future suffered a setback. I assure you if Tota Ram had been given a chance he would have been a brilliant writer. He would have been a genius, a celebrity, a veritable leader of men. But Tota Ram had to stay on in the village. But he was so preoccupied by the idea of time and the futility of his one wasted life in general, plus all the wasted lives of others, that he wanted to do something positive. He wanted to impress upon the village people the value of time, so what does he do for it? Well, our Tota Ram is no native fool so he goes to the city and buys a brass gong and a wooden hammer. He hangs the gong in his top bedroom window and strikes the hour hard so that everyone can hear the time. And every day, for the past twenty-nine years, no matter what Tota Ram has been doing or where he has been, he always regularly, without fail, strikes the hour.'

'Tota Ram's time is always wrong. Yesterday he was ten minutes fast, and today he is ten minutes slow.'

'That doesn't matter Vijay, what matters is the certainty, the stubbornness and the doggedness of purpose he has. He is determined to make the village people conscious of time. Now you may remember Tota Ram had a little orchard.'

'Yes, where we stole the guavas and they were all bitter and raw. Vijay and his friend kicked all the unripe guavas and pushed them in the gutter.'

'Never mind about the guavas but listen. Tota Ram had all the trees cut down. He sold his orchard, land and the trees for one single aim, and that was to collect enough money to build a real clock tower. Such was his dedication, such was his philanthropy. He went to all the wealthy landlords and Brahmins for donations but they would not give him a paisa, and they conveniently forgot that they set all their mental clocks and watches by Tota Ram's clock. "Why, Dada, we are sorry, we have no cash. By the way, the sound of your gong doesn't really reach us." Everyone made some excuse and Tota Ram got no financial help with his project. In the end he collected every paisa he had and bought that narrow square of land near the old Khookha Gate. Now he has successfully completed a three-storey tower. It is true that the building is of little merit. It is badly constructed, dark, and ugly. It might fall down within a decade or two. But it is the reality of Tota Ram's dream. He has lived to make it come true. Have you noticed that he is nearing seventy and still he persists on going up twelve times a day on those dark, dingy, unlit stairs to strike the hour? Why, he could fall down and break his neck, and there are so many pigeons nesting there, but despite all these difficulties he still carries on. Now there is a man for you to emulate. He has had an aim which he has nearly fulfilled.'

'Tota Ram's clock tower has no clocks. Instead it has four big round eyes, and each round eye has six pigeons in it. They flutter and squawk, filling the tower with snowy feathers and sticky bird droppings. Tota Ram has no money for the clocks!'

'That is of no importance. The important thing is that the man has done what he set out to do.'

Vijay went to our father's school when he was ten and Asha was left alone. She did not have much to say to Shanta who always sat at home and knitted. But Asha loved the wild, she loved the company of trees, the wind and the dusty roads. She was happier climbing a tree than being at home. Her wanderings and nomadic life became uncontrollable and her mother had to do something about it. She had not done any systematic studies after running away from school, but had read voraciously, indiscriminately and at random anything that came her way from old newspapers to old mythology, *Mahabharata, Ramayana,* the Scriptures, *Upnishadas,* and anything else she could lay her hands on. Her English reading consisted of Shakespeare's tragedies, *Pilgrim's Progress, Paradise Lost* and the complete works of Charles Dickens and Thackeray. Her father had painstakingly taught her English with grammar and syntax on his daily visits to the fields to bring fodder for the cattle, and she was quick to retain everything. Her memory was so sharp that she could recite what she had learnt the previous day verbatim, much to the surprise of her father. She did not understand these works comprehensively but she read them all the same. She liked reading aloud and memorising bits of passages and then singing them like songs. She seemed reasonably happy with this unstructured existence. But one day her mother told her to get ready and she was taken to a private academy. Her hair had now grown long and thick again. She missed Vijay and was lonely so she was prepared to try this academy. The Girls' Progressive College, as it was called, was housed in a two-roomed, derelict brickhouse which at one time belonged to a well-to-do Muslim shopkeeper. It stood at the end of some very rough streets. The streets always smelt of stale blood and leather. Butchers and shoemakers lived there. They had to pass through these Untouchable quarters, and the boys in the narrow alleyways would hang around and gape at their fine clothes with great amazement and generally ogle them. There was also a bully boy in the street. He was part of a gang who shouted obscenities and made lewd jokes. The bully's hands were rough and covered with sores, and his face was generally unwashed. His hair was dusty and matted. He looked like a mean, stray dog.

One day, as Asha was going up the street alone, he caught her by both hands and stared at her. At close quarters his eyes looked piggish and sore, and his breath smelt of stale cigarettes and raw onions. Many Harijan boys collected stubs from the roadside and started smoking them to appear grown up. Asha's arms were aching and hurting but he would not let her go. He kept on whispering, 'Show me that flower between your legs and give me a kiss.' Asha did not understand what he was talking about. She kicked and cried but despite his leanness the boy was muscular and strong, and then he kissed her mouth hard with his rubbery, smoky lips. Asha went to school numb, bewildered and feeling guilty as if in some mysterious way she had invited the boy to perform this deed on her person. She never went to school alone after that.

The teacher was an unmarried girl. She had a round face, full of pimples, and high cheekbones. She wore glasses and her deep-set, round eyes peered out of them with great intensity. She looked like an owl. She was probably the only girl in the village who had finished high school. She knew some English and used obscure vocabulary which Asha couldn't always understand. She gave Asha some books to read more suited to her years. She made a presentation to her of a book entitled *The Blue Bird* and Asha read it so many times that she could relate it word for word without looking at it. The teacher was hoping to get married soon and was using her time to earn some money for her dowry. She divided her pupils into two groups, advanced and intermediate, and Asha was put in the advanced group. There were no more than a dozen girls in both groups, and they were the ones whose parents were sufficiently interested in higher education in the whole village...

There were only four girls in our class, Peely, Sheely, Kunti and myself. And in the other, Bansee, Teemee, Gianee, Sudesh, Raksha and three others who attended now and again.

Bansee and Teemee were much older and keen to learn, and the rest of them just came for the sake of gossip and fun. Gianee was lame but nevertheless very strong and later on I had to suffer quite a lot at her hands. Bansee gave up when the school closed down but Teemee went to the city to carry on her education. There she met a lover and wanted to marry him. But he was from a lower caste than hers. Worse, some of the village hooligans thought of her relationship as an insult to the village. So the 'mob' kept a close watch on her movements for a week or so. One day they caught her and the boyfriend in a compromising position. They beat the young man into a pulp and left him with broken ribs and almost dead. Through all this Teemee kept crying and shouting helplessly but nobody went to their aid. After that all types of sinister stories were spread about her in the village. Her parents put an end to this premature freedom by marrying her off in a hurry to an ugly old widower. When she returned to the village she had a different appearance. She used to be a beautiful girl with a cream, rosebud complexion. Now she was pale and haggard looking and had sunken cheeks, but she had a nice voice and recited poetry at special functions. I recall one occasion when she marched up to the stage, but the meeting was so crowded that she had stage-fright and her voice broke down, and all the assembled boys giggled. But it was not like Teemee to accept defeat: she went up a second time and read the poem beautifully. But that was all in the past for her now, the end of all her dreams. She must exist now as a shadow to an old man and his family.

Peely was not beautiful. She was dark-skinned. She had blue-black lips and very white teeth. She looked like a dark pony with her hair in a pony tail which jumped up and down on her back like a fluffy, unkempt, short bob. She had big brown eyes, the only beautiful feature of her face, her ears protruded, and she had a long nose. So she had a horsey look rather than a human appearance. She had a horse's laughter too; it was much more like prolonged neighing than laughing. She had big feet which she rarely put into shoes, and big, flat, pancake hands which were rough and harsh to touch. She talked through her nose and always smelt of garlic. She also consumed great quantities of raw sugar cane which she chewed and munched during recess, and gave great loud belches much to the amusement of the rest of the class.

I came to make her acquaintance when I was twelve. I went to the academy with my sister and was left scowling at a very narrow, dingy room which had a variety of strong smells coming out of it. There was the sickly smell of rose water coming from the teacher's direction, and there was also the smell of pickles and onions brought by the pupils in their packed lunches. The little room seemed to be packed with big girls. In fact it seemed to be spilling over with big, strapping girls. I was just about to turn and flee home – my usual route of escape – when someone touched my elbow and said, 'You can come in and sit with me. I'll make room for you. What's your name?'

'Asha. What is yours?'

'Peely.' So in I squeezed and crouched down in a corner on a rush mat which she had brought from home. At recess we shared our food. She gave me a tasty bit of pickled cauliflower, sweet matthi (cake), and melon. I in turn gave her the only things I had brought, my aloo parathas (potato bread). We ran around in the yard, threw stones, chased each other and wrestled. At the end of the day she took me to her home which was en route to my house. It was a little old house with very dark rooms, and each room was lower than the other with the result that I tripped over and broke my new glass bangle, and cut my wrist. At once, Peely came to the rescue and attended to it with a wad of cottonwool. The house had no bathroom in it, no water and no toilet. The courtyard was partitioned off with a low mud wall which was obviously built by her mother. This was the place they called the 'kitchen'. It had a hearth in it and a basket of dung-cakes for fuel. I thought her mother would have cooked the evening meal for Peely to eat now but there were no signs of a meal. Peely seemed to know all about cooking. She put her satchel down and went straight in to cook for the whole family. She had difficulty in lighting the fire with the cakes; her eyes became red with smoke and her little wisps of hair smelt of smoke. As she blew again and again into the dying embers, she got thoroughly exhausted and fell into a fit of coughing. Then her mother came out of a dark, cell-like room; she walked so quietly and slowly that she seemed like a creeping apparition. She told Peely in a low but very firm voice to put a paraffin-soaked rag on to the embers as she had told her so many times, and then try again. The old woman was thin and yellow and I thought that the name 'Peely' (yellow) should have suited her so much better than her daughter who was anything but pale. The mother's face was woven out of closely set wrinkles and she was skeletal. Her breath sounded hollow and it seemed as if she was drawing it with all her force and then pulling it in, in the same manner. Her mummified breasts rose up and down as she breathed and talked in a quiet whisper. The woman was so much like a ghost and frightening to look at, but she had, nice, cool, gentle, smiling eyes. She was very sparing with words; it may be that it hurt her to speak. And as soon as the fire got under way she withdrew into her cell-like room again. Peely told me that her mother was an invalid, and had always suffered from consumption.

There was something ancient and morbid about the whole house. It smelt of stored corn and sweet, raw molasses. It had more flies and ants than other houses but that was not the sole reason that the house looked depressing. It was as if all the efforts made by sunlight and fresh air to enter were deliberately blocked. All the ventilators were bricked up, all the windows covered with black blinds, and the only door to the house had four sets of locks on it. It was also hung with a thick black blanket, so that even when the door was open the blind was there. It effectively shut out all sources of light, air and sun. It was more like a tomb than a house, and the woman sat in her cell like a ghost. The atmosphere seemed strange and unnatural. This was not the house of a city dweller, this was not the house of a businessman, this was not the house of some crank but of a farmer whose family were used to spending two-thirds of their lives in the fields.

Then Peely's father came home. Peely served him the food before she sat down to eat with me. He looked like one of his own strong bullocks. He was like Peely but even more of an animal in his build and looks. He was a small man, very widely built with broad shoulders. He had a snub nose and deep-set eyes. His beard was thick but it scattered and spread in all directions. He wore no trousers but a brief sheet was wrapped around and tied on his hips, and he wore an open-necked, home-made shirt. His wife came demurely out of her cell; her head was wrapped in a duppatta, as now was Peely's. I thought the man might demand for me to have my head wrapped similarly but I had no duppatta with me. But the old man, who was very like a bull calf or a gorilla, did not notice me at all and went on chewing his food. He snatched a piece of chapatti, dipped it in dal, hurriedly thrusting it in his mouth, and it was hardly down when he grabbed some more to push it in again. It seemed as if an invisible person was after his food, so if he did not get to it first, it might be taken away from him. And all the while the man made no attempt to talk. The woman kept fidgeting in the room and rearranging the brass pots. He scowled at her but kept absolutely quiet. The pots were all polished and dusted and lay in straight rows over a wooden box. But the woman went on fidgeting and wiping them and rewiping them with the end of her duppatta, and then rearranging them in straight lines once more. It was as if she was playing at being busy until the man found his tongue and some words to tell her something. But after his meal he just grunted, belched, yawned, stretched and stood up. At his uncouth performance she screwed up her nose to show her distaste but did not say anything. The man stood up, took some water in the palm of his cupped hands, gargled with a splash, spat in the open drain then went into a dark room. He reappeared loaded with a huge sack of wheat. He carried it like a toy on his broad shoulders. Peely opened the door for him and he was gone, with his bare feet making big wet marks all over the floor. Peely's mother turned around, her eyes were gentle and smiling once more; she wiped the floor, sighed and after this operation she looked apologetically at me as if to say 'don't mind my husband's manners, he is not quite human!' and then she was gone again into the dark recesses of her cell.

All the while Peely was silent but from time to time she smiled and reassured me that everything was going to be fine. Then she climbed up on a string and bamboo ladder and beckoned me to follow her. She was still demurely wrapped in her duppatta from head to shoulders so that her bosom did not show. Here was a little room overlooking the street. The windows also had black blinds on them but Peely drew them back with a scornful jerk and the room was full of bright evening sunshine, warm and friendly. Peely showed me her treasures in beads and bracelets; she also showed me how to do tricks with her thumb, dislocate it and make it stick out at an angle, wobble and do funny tricks, and we both fell into hysterical, side-splitting laughter, but then suddenly Peely went all quiet, self-conscious and ashamed and I did not know the reason why. A guilty look came over her face, and she beat the pillows with her huge fists until it hurt her knuckles and she swore under her breath. Then from a distance came her mother's faint, whining voice, 'Peely, I heard you laughing. How many times have I asked you not to laugh loudly? It is not good manners for genteel girls to laugh so loud. You should just smile and that's enough. Your laughter is uncultured and rude, and woe is me, everyone in the street would have heard it! Come down. It is time to go to the farm.' Peely looked embarrassed and furious. She bit her lower lip and it bled. She did not like to be insulted in front of me. So she grew angry with me and twisted my arms and it hurt me. I nearly cried, then she told me to get out and that she did not want to see me any more. I ran all the way back home.

At night as I lay in bed I thought of her, her dark home, her strange mother and bullish father till I saw all of them in the darkness of the night. I was scared so I shut my eyes tight, repeated the *Gayatri Mantra* that I knew by heart, over and over again till I was asleep.

OF FATHERS AND FRIENDS

The sun was high up when Asha's father shouted for her. Asha jumped out of bed and looked at the clock, it was only six, and she was angry at her father. To placate her he pulled funny faces and sang her favourite song. She forgot about being angry and started singing with him. After the song she realised that she had been again fooled by him but she could not stay angry any longer. She ate her bread and butter, drank a glass of lassi and went out of doors with her satchel. On the way she stopped by the side of the pond and threw pebbles in it. When the pebbles skimmed the surface circular ripples went round and round, and they stretched a long way till the pebble went to the bottom. Then a depression was left in the middle, and some air bubbles came up. She saw a man wash a buffalo at the far end, and she went around to the side. She knew that the pond was full of leeches and the man was standing in the water. He was sure to have some on his legs. When the man came out, sure enough, he had many leeches clinging to his legs. He stamped his feet and some fell down, some he pulled away himself and crushed them with his stick, and the blood was all over the grass and his legs were striped with blood. But there was still another clinging to the inside of his leg. It was growing fatter by the minute. When the man saw it, he quickly tugged at it and caught it in his hand. He did not seem to be afraid but rather amused; he laughed a short snort and then squeezed the leech in his hand and the blood came pouring and rolling, rushing and dripping in a red torrent, and the leech lay there on the bank like a still, dry leaf. Asha felt sick in her stomach, the bread and the lassi stuck in her throat, and she ran off to school. On the way she saw two boys fighting. They both had nice white shirts on and striped shorts. They looked like twin brothers. But they splashed mud at each other and then put their satchels down and kicked each other. They chased each other in ever diminishing circles; their eyes were screwed up and looked like pinheads. Then one of them jumped on the other and they both rolled in the dust, alternating the winning, on-top position. They shouted abuse at each other. One said the other was a son of a bitch; the other shouted he was 'dogbred' too and so on and so on. In the end one of them got up and pulled the other's hair. By now their clothes were heavily stained and dark-brown, splashed with mud, and their neatly parted hair looked like a jungle. Soon the fight ceased as unceremoniously as it had begun, and they were once again on their way to school. They now kicked at stones, at dust, at flying paper and at each other.

Asha resumed her journey. When she reached the schoolroom the sun was high up and it was hot. But the door was still locked and no one was around so she sat down on the doorstep, took a ball of tamarind, a pinch of salt and chilli powder from a little bottle. She sprinkled these on pieces of tamarind and popped them in her mouth like sweets. The tamarind was sour and sharp and the mixture of chilli powder burnt her tongue and made her eyes water. This was a new habit which she had acquired from one of the big girls. She spat the stones out all over the place. She hit a stray dog with a stone and it whimpered and went away whining. She heard Tota Ram's clock tower strike nine, so she got up and threw the rest of the tamarind in the gutter. It was forbidden to chew it in school.

Gradually other girls appeared and waited for the door to be unlocked. They stood in twos and threes chattering. They were all big girls and had lots of interesting things to talk about to each other but they never took Asha into their confidence, and she was left alone and restless, standing in a corner. Time passed and there was no sign of the teacher. So one of the girls went to her home to fetch the keys. This type of episode was almost an everyday occurrence: the teacher rarely appeared before ten as it was a private school, and nobody checked. The girls unlocked the door, armed themselves with brooms and buckets of water, and started sweeping up yesterday's rubbish while others put a map up on the wall, took the daily register out of the cupboard and dusted the desks. They kept themselves occupied till the teacher came and then they fawned on her to win her favour. They brought her bunches of marigolds, vegetables and other tit-bits their mothers could spare. This was to achieve a good 'pass' in return for their daughters' labours. These certificates issued by the teacher were not recognised but the mothers treasured them as it gave the girls greater value in the marriage market. Some girls were not at all interested in studies, could not spell their family names but still obtained these certificates. There was one such girl. Her name was Sudesh but everyone called her Devi. She dressed in an untidy fashion, had big yellow teeth and smelt unwashed. But her people were well-off and she was the only daughter. She was slow, lazy and not at all interested in learning. When, after five years' attendance, she failed to grasp correctly the techniques of writing and spelt her father's name wrong, the father felt that something was sadly amiss somewhere. So he decided to approach the teacher with some of his wealth: the girl was awarded a good pass and issued with a certificate written in gold lettering. She was then married into a wealthy family with a lot of fuss and a splash of money. It was said that her wedding was the only occasion when her father bought himself a pair of shoes.

The Frog said to the Horse 'Be careful, don't step on me. The grass on the verges is good but so is my house where I live with my assembly of wives.'

The Horse said, 'You're a frog, and you are an insignificant little creature, and your body is soft like dough. I can go anywhere, and eat any grass I fancy. You're not my keeper but I am yours. I can crush you if I wish.'

There stood a hairy Langoor scratching under the tree and listening to this chatter. He moved slowly and deliberately towards the horse, and he flung out at the four legs of the horse, therefore making him tumble, and walked away again chewing a sugar cane stick and life went on.

Peely was dying to speak to Asha. Asha brought her own mat now and always sat in a corner. She no longer sat on Peely's mat. Peely grinned whenever she got a chance, and her grin was that of a horse. At dinner time she opened many wrapped-up parcels and brought out barfi (a fudge-like sweet), fried parathas and papdums. She held these goodies up to Asha whose mouth watered and all her resistance melted away, and she was with Peely once more. No matter how often they quarrelled they could never stay away from each other. Peely's mother was sick so Peely ran the house. She made trips to the farm with heavy baskets on her head before breakfast and before coming to school. The farm was miles outside the village and she generally returned laden with mustard shoots and turnips. She was always late for school. Asha went to her house every day to accompany her to school. But she was busy doing grown-up chores and rushing around. Then she would snatch herself a stale chapatti with butter and a lump of molasses. Every day her diet was the same and Asha gaped to see the speed at which she gulped it down.

Peely had three brothers all married and living away. She had an older sister, too, who was married but not happily, so she stayed at home most of the time. Yet the sister did not assist Peely. She, too, was very strict with Peely. Once Asha saw her tell Peely off for letting go of her duppatta, and running with an uncovered bosom in the presence of some old men. This was on the way to school when old men generally congregated and sat on a ledge by the roadside. Asha was with Peely and they were having a race. Peely was annoyed. Her brown eyes sparkled like a tiger's, and she went on kicking her feet till they were bruised and sore. Peely was very basic in her emotions. If she was pleased or upset she expressed herself much as a monkey would do. In this respect she reminded Asha very much of her father.

'You are lucky,' said Peely's mother. 'Your parents are educated. But I am struggling hard to educate her father, who you know is illiterate. He does not like educated girls. He says they start writing love messages to boys, and it all ends up bad. But Peely is a good girl.

She has been brought up in a good home. She is a child but I can trust her. It is different with you.' The old woman smiled, coughed, paused and resumed. Her eyes were sad but they flickered with a brilliance. She looked like a witch in the dark, in the sweet, sugary smell of her hermit cell. She reminded Asha of Coleridge's Geraldine.

'My people are all city people,' she resumed. 'They value education. I was brought up in a different culture. Yes, they were respectable folk. They knew how to maintain their dignity and their Izzat. This is a little village and there is no privacy here.' Saying this, she jerked the blind tighter still so that it was even darker in the room. Now in the gloom her faint rhapsody of a voice sounded, hollow, tired and bitter, as she condemned the street, the village, including her husband.

Asha talked to Peely about the conversation she had had with her mother. Peely just laughed and shrugged her shoulders. Gradually, Asha came to know that the woman had married beneath her. Her brothers had good ranks in the army and were wealthy people. They were literate and cultured while her husband was just the opposite. He was coarse and illiterate and did not appreciate education. This made Peely's mother introspective and negative. She shut herself away and gradually made herself believe that she was tubercular, and became an invalid. She darkened the house because that was the only way she could express her rejection of her life-style and other people.

Peely said, 'Asha. Let us go to our farm. We have got a new tubewell fitted now. It works with electricity. I will give you oranges and melons if you come with me.' The farm had a little brick house built near the well. It had a little bed in the verandah and there were marigolds growing in small tubs, and the little champak bushes were loaded with flowers. The marigolds had a spicy smell around them as they shook their little pom-pom heads in the breeze. On the charpoy lay a boy of fifteen reading a newspaper. He made no attempt to get up or make room for them. So Asha kept on observing. There were rows of tomato plants in a plot nearby and the plants were spice-scented and laden with fruit. Some were bright red, some yellow, some green tinged with gold, and some all green, and their ripening smell was being wafted in the breeze. A man was pulling radishes and turnips up. Peely felt very proud to be giving a guided tour to Asha, and she showed her all the sights she felt would interest her. She showed her the fluffy chickens in a pen; she showed her the orange and lemon groves. She showed her the sky-high sugar cane fields and lectured her on the various types of sugar cane they grew. Then she took her to a low, thatched room from which fragrant and pungent smells came in great profusion. In that room there was a cauldron of gigantic proportions resting on a pit fixed to the ground, and a man sat beside this pit with a huge iron fork. He sat by a huge pile of dried sugar cane after the juice had been extracted from it. Every now and then he pushed a bundle of these leavings in the pit, and a strong fire burnt and crackled merrily under the bubbling cauldron. The cauldron was full of sugar cane juice which was now thickening into a custard and a man was scraping and stirring it with a giant iron spatula. Another man clad in stained and dirty clothes was collecting all the scum from the juice and was ladling it into a bucket. Asha was told that he was a Harijan labourer who would take this bucket of scum off the juice and then his wife would cook some rice in it for the family supper. Peely said, 'It is precious for them and they live on it and rice during this season.'

'But it is dirty and full of impurities!' said Asha.

'It is money to them. Anyway we don't ask him for any money,' replied Peely. Now the bubbling substance had turned into a coarse, grain-like mixture. The men carefully moved the cauldron to one side and with a large, spoon-like wooden spatula they dished this mixture in little lumps on to a calico sheet. And this was gur (dumpling sugar) as they called it. Peely ate these lumps by the dozen but they were very sweet, sticky and sickly.

Later on, Peely took Asha to the tubewell and called the boy who lounged on the charpoy. He appeared and started climbing down the deep well very nimbly. There was a narrow ladder running down the deep recesses of the well, and soon he disappeared into the darkness much to Asha's concern. Later he came up after attending to some machinery and turned the electric switch on. The water came in torrents. It was magic, enchanting and mesmerising to watch. No bullocks were required to go round and the water ran in great waterfalls at the touch of a mere button. It was soporific to watch it gush and flow in such vast quantities. Peely pushed her big feet under the spout and Asha followed suit. The water was warm and clear and it fell on their feet producing strong and strange exhilarations and tickling their legs. When it was dusk Peely cut a very large water melon open. There was no knife so she just banged it on a stone and broke it into manageable chunks. Asha ate it greedily, dipping her whole face and letting juice plaster her thoroughly. To see the mess Asha got herself into, everyone laughed, including the unsociable boy, and Peely laughed loud and long sounding just like a neighing horse. She managed to eat four pieces to Asha's one.

Dr Kashmiri Lal Sharma, MD, was one of the new arrivals in the village. People were suspicious, and as he sat in his one-roomed shop, with a huge, garish sign over the shop front, they stared at him, watched him, eavesdropped on him but did not go in. The village did not possess any qualified doctors but there were plenty of quacks, and their profession generally flourished. There was the son of a barber who was much patronised; he could suggest a cure from a pimple to a serious tumour. Nothing was beyond his medical knowledge, and when things got out of hand, the knife was always handy! He also did abortions on young unmarried girls who got into difficulties, usually at night to hide their shame, but not until he was very well paid for his labours. Of course, some died and were hurriedly cremated at midnight before the police could be informed. They were only girls, they said, and the whole village entered into a conspiracy of silence to preserve their honour and the Izzat of their white beards as the village elders put it. Gradually, on this wealth, he built himself a bigger practice and an even bigger house. He always dressed immaculately in white and often paraded the streets late at night.

But Dr Kashmiri Lal was a relative stranger. Nobody knew his past, and like a stranger he was kept at bay, watched and monitored carefully, and criticised for what he wore, the way he walked and talked. He had a one-roomed workshop where he mixed his own medicines; half a dozen bottles stood on a dusty shelf with boric acid taking up a prominent position among them. He would arrive early in the morning, sweep around his shop, polish the newly acquired signboard and sit down, expectantly, to read the paper. He always had the air of a very busy person although he had next to nothing to do. He brought with him two younger brothers, his mother and father, and a wife.

They had all come from Pakistan and were in the process of resettling. Now, Dr Kashmiri Lal Sharma had not been born in

Kashmir: in fact, it is debatable whether his parents knew there was such a place. He was named after the State because the parents liked the sound of the word: it seemed prestigious, aristocratic, distant and enchanting. But Dr Kashmiri Lal singularly lacked any enchantment. He was a painfully thin, spotty and square-jawed young man, and when he walked his long arms hung limply by his side and his legs did not seem to co-ordinate. He looked more like a feather-ruffled scarecrow with a crow-like, beaky nose and intense eyes. He was ugly, scraggy and small and talked in an affected manner as if he was highly educated and privileged. It is very likely that his education was patchy, and the knowledge of medicine he professed was acquired from paperbacks. Nevertheless, he had a convincing bedside manner. Gradually people came to accept him and the number of bottles on his counter increased. He also bought himself a mixing machine, and put out rows and rows of a face cream called 'Sharma Snow'. It appeared to have its base in talc mixed with coconut oil and whoever used it found her face covered in dry, flaking skin. So the product never had a big market even though he gave out free samples.

Then he brought out Sharma Jasmine Perfume – 'a perfume that rejuvenates weak hearts and makes you young again'. Sharma Jasmine Oil – 'with that magic in it that will make your bald crown glow with rich black hair'. He also advertised that he could cure many 'private illnesses' both of males and females including 'impotence'. His products never sold on a national basis but they were new to the village and everyone bought a jar or two to try so that the doctor could now afford brilliant, white, professional, western clothes. His lean, hungry face acquired a look of satisfaction and his thin body started to grow round.

The first time Raju tried Dr Kashmiri Lal's skill was when his daughter Asha was ill. He was allowed to give penicillin injections to the girl. He diluted the mixture to obtain four injections out of one dose as he was paid by the number of injections he administered. Soon the girl's bottom was like a pin cushion and she could not sit on it for weeks. But it was a golden opportunity for the doctor to make money. He was also called upon to sit by Asha's side and administer glucose and water every hour to combat dehydration, but he thought, as the child was dying in any case, why bother? So, during the long night, whenever he saw her growing restless he just moistened her lips with a finger dipped in the solution. The next morning the ailing child not only had a very high fever due to lack of liquids but a very inflamed throat. She could neither cry nor make a sound, nor swallow. And when he was asked when she would show a sign of improvement his stock reply was 'slowly, slowly'. In the end the Master Ji grew so frustrated and angry that he lifted him bodily from the chair he was lounging in, and threw him out in the street.

Of course, when his daughter Asha got well again relations improved, and the doctor always sought credit for saving her life. He was also called upon to treat sick cows, ailing buffaloes and their progeny. Sometimes his treatment failed and the ailing creatures died but the doctor was not to blame, for in the end it was all in God's hands, and just their misfortune. He grew so famous that he was called to help the village midwife at difficult deliveries. The midwife was from a Harijan caste and had low standards of hygiene. Sometimes in emergencies she dispensed with scrubbing her hands as soap and hot water were not always readily available. In such conditions many women died with their young ones or during the process of giving birth. But with the arrival of the new doctor people's minds grew more restful and many a woman had an easy delivery. It was not that the doctor was profusely knowledgeable about gynaecology, it was just his magic presence and the magic powders which he gave to the pain-blinded women. However, the rate in stillbirths did not markedly improve nor the deaths of women in childbirth. But it was never the doctor's fault: after all he was not God, and one could not change one's fate which was stamped in indelible ink by God from birth.

When Asha was well she often went to the doctor's surgery and watched him treat conjunctivitis and inflamed eyes with zinc drops, dress sores and wounds with nondescript medicines which were hardly effective and yet people crowded in. He had now also acquired a social circle which was composed mainly of young village men, layabouts, dandies and gossipmongers, with the result that ordinary people held him in awe and respect. After all, he had such powerful friends who could abduct their daughters any time of the day at the nod of his head.

The doctor's eyes nowadays, when he looked at Asha, would assume an odd look and he had a queer smile at the corners of his mouth which made Asha feel uneasy. He certainly was getting 'odd' thought Asha. He waited till his surgery was empty and then he would call Asha to the desk and with an excuse to examine her he would start fiddling with her stomach and his fingers would gradually creep up and up towards her small, growing breasts. It was a strange thing to do since it made the doctor's face red and his chest heaved up and down noisily. Asha felt like giggling but was also scared. Then the doctor's hands would start traversing down and down towards her pants till she could stand it no longer and jumped away. She came mainly to collect magazines and colourful pamphlets which the doctor had by the dozen and some of which he would give to her. The books had strange, incomprehensible stories in them. Stories about women talking in a strange language and men behaving in a funny manner. They were not the kind of books a child could understand and yet she read them all spellbound for they had a mystery in them she wished to fathom.

Then one day her father said, 'Come, let us see what you are reading?' But when he looked at them his face went purple with anger and he started stomping, shouting and swearing, 'Why the Devil, I would murder him with my bare hands. How dare he give such filth to young children?' He shouted many other profanities, put his shoes on and rushed away with the pile of magazines. Asha followed him. The doctor's little room was full of people but her father did not wait for the people to clear. He went straight up to the doctor, held him by his neck and shook him, and then he slapped his face hard. He was so angry that he could not speak and instead, very dramatically, he tore all his books to pieces and threw them on the floor. The village people just sat there with their faces stone-like, expressionless and vacant. Much to Asha's sadness she was never allowed to visit Doctor Kashmiri Lal Sharma again and she could never decide whether he was her friend or enemy.

PART TWO

In the dark, rainy night, when the only light was provided by the lightning which flashed every now and then, we lay together in a little room. I was a little shivering fledgling and you were big, warm and soft, and at my constant demands for unravelling fathomless details and stories you sought to amuse me, and you told me endless fables, tales and stories. You told me stories of misfits like Darshan, stories of outcasts and stories of grand revenge and great meanness, and you also told me your own story – the best of all the stories. I, an ignorant, forgetful child, I who cannot even recall how you looked and how I looked as a child, how could I have otherwise peeped at your past except through you, and tried to experience how things had been before my day when you were a child?

All the sadness is ours – the daughters and sons of a lonely Manu contemplating life after the great Flood – and all the joys can be ours too if we love and live without changing our basic selves. Time passes and so do we and neither of them can be called back again. After all your stories I realise how little I know of your life and times. After all the tales your mother told you, how little you know of the life that was hers. It is sad, it is very sad, and yet irrevocable. You can name half a dozen of your forefathers, all males, yet how little you can tell me about them. And of the women and the lives of women you know nothing. They gave birth to all those men and yet they stayed anonymous, hardly worth recording. The male ancestors, too, are now just a string of names, and they may easily have been tokens, but they lived, they all had lives like yours. They had houses, little children and big hopes, and yet all is forgotten, is gone forever. Their lives were ordinary so they are not a part of history which is largely made up of famous people. And yet, you say that to be born a Brahmin is the greatest honour God can bestow on you? Our male ancestors – all Brahmins – they do not even form a part of man's evolution for we know all that is worth knowing. They are gone forever. Their children must have roamed the streets of our

ancient village, and women must have picked cotton like Grandmother. Their wives must have sat in the winter sun and spun.
They must have had deaths and marriages in their families. But
who knows about them? They are dead and with them is cremated
the time in which they lived and moved. You, even as the most
wonderful, wizardly storyteller, cannot really tell me a story about
them because it happened before your time. And you pride yourself
for remembering a string of names of my male ancestors – women
do not figure at all. I wonder if the sun was hotter when they lived
in the village? I wonder if all of them lived in the same ancestral
home where Grandmother lives, and where she says she sees the
ghost of my Grandfather seated on a black stallion? I wonder if they
had floods like we had the other year when it rained and rained for
seven whole days? I wonder if their women were beautiful? I
wonder where they all came from? You say that one of our ancestors
was the great philosopher of Vedic times who wrote the famous
treatise, the *Sankhya Darshana,* but what can you tell me about the
others after him, and more of the recent past? Our life is just like a
flickering candle: when the candle goes out there is nothing left, no,
not even a shadow but the darkness, and all else is gone except the
darkness. Our past is oblivion forever. Mother goes and worships
our forefathers' shrines, empty tombs like our Grandmother did
before her. Women perpetuating the memory of the males of the
family. They celebrate the unknown ancestors and declare that they
can feel their presence. But there is nothing there of them, nor of
their times save the hidden crows' nests and snakes in the thickets.
Now mother gives them milk to drink and rice to eat. She does not
even know if they were well fed when they lived. No, sadly, they are
gone forever, and unlike the Muslims not even a graveyard holds their
memory. Their bones are finite sand in the vast bed of the Ganges,
and their veins, marrow and sinew perished with them. Their
memories are extinct except for half a dozen names chanted like a
mantra. Who knows if they writhe and groan in your supposed
heaven or hell and grin stupidly at the aimlessness and futility of
human existence and of their own? Who knows, there might not be
anything left of them? Maybe the heaven and hell of human
existence is on this earth alone, and when we die we die forever, our

breath kissing the wind and blowing away with it. This is the strange story, the strange enigma, of human life, time and death. We live, we eat, we breathe, and our lives spin like a circle around an invisible object called time. The clocks everlastingly tick; yet time with 'everlasting' is a contradiction: while the day changes into night, the night into dawn, then daylight again. These changes are regular and we know time passes.

From little children, we grow into inflexible grown-ups and have our own little children, then die, thus completing the cycle, and all the time we carry invisible time clocks in our invisible pockets till it is all spent, and we prepare to die and complete the circle. That is how it was for them – this is how it will be for you and me. We shall all tell our little tales and pass away, and nothing shall be left of us except time and the earth which will weather all things and stay like the rock it is made out of long after us, with secrets and time past in its bosom. This is a strange tale of living and dying.

FATHER TELLS THE BEST STORY

The story I am going to tell you is the story of my life. I think this story will prove to be more interesting and realistic than a story from a book or one I make up for you.

My mother had gone to attend a wedding at her mother's. And one rainy night in the month of January, twenty-one days gone, the year was 1905, people in the house heard the cries of a child, and there was my mother holding me upside down. She later told me that I was not expected for some days and I had come into the world too early. I believe she was right. I was the youngest of three brothers but also had a sister younger than me. We have never understood each other well, although I have been fond of her. There were other children before me but they did not survive. There is a big age difference between your uncle Ram and me. We have never been fond, but tolerant enough, of each other. He is quiet, diplomatic and noncommittal. You can never tell what his real thoughts are, then he comes out with a profound, sarcastic remark about the nature of things. He spits each word out most methodic-ally, and then falls into silence again. He is the uncle who lives in the hills. His wife suffers from mental aberrations if he comes down to the plains, so he stays there – up in the hills. I have often told him that the hills have made him lose all his feelings and now he is a stone. We stayed with him when we took Shanta for her operation. It was a terrible experience. You could never get a word out of the man. It was grey, lonely and raining all the time. Your aunt always wanted to know how many chapattis we each wanted to eat so that she could cook to measure. Why, it was impossible, how could I measure my appetite beforehand? Anyway, one day she cooked a panful of porridge and it tasted bitter and stale. When I examined it closely it had dead wheat weevils in it. I was sick right away. But your uncle ate it all up, saying 'It all costs money, Raju, and in the hills everything is doubly dear.' He is a skinflint and he would suck a fly for its juice if he could. I was glad to get away, and the mad woman kept going on and shouting at me, 'Remember how you all beat me with mulberry canes. I was only twelve when I came to your house; I had no mother and you all beat me up most cruelly with saplings and canes. I yelled and cried but you dogs, you didn't take any notice. You and your brothers were always callous, and I curse you all.' Well, honestly, I don't remember a thing about beating her with mulberry canes. Evidently, she has made herself believe that everyone had fun torturing and tormenting her. She believes we are all her enemies except Babu Ji, your uncle. She is a mental case. I never wish to stay with them again. It was just God damn, bloody murder.

Now, to come back to my early years. I am told that I suckled my mother's breast until I was five. I think it was very silly of her to let me carry on. I also used to sing songs in praise of Lord Krishna to the bells of her spinning wheel. One day, when quite young, I was playing with Babu Jheer (low caste water bearer). When it grew late Babu's mother took me home and my mother took in Babu. They suckled us both for a couple of days. Sometimes, I wonder if I am still Babu and Babu me? We don't look very much alike now, but we may have done then, of course. I wonder what would have become of me if I had stayed Babu? I suppose I would have carried full pitchers on my shoulders for the rest of my life.

I played Guli Danda (tip cat) where our house is now – then it used to be all fields. I never wore any shoes nor a shirt until I went to the high school. I worked in the fields from a very young age. I sowed, I hoed and weeded, cut stacks of millet, and even helped my mother pick cotton. I also played ball in the street; the ball was always made by my mother. It was a plain ball of rags wrapped around in cotton and then securely embroidered with the needle into different coloured squares. It was a work of art and very tough – the rag and the cotton never came apart.

When I was four or five I started going to school. The school was an open-air one, no building, nor any rooms, just a ploughed field with a few trees around it. The teacher squatted regally on a raised, mud-plastered platform on a hessian mat. Me and the rest of the boys sat on the earth on our bare bottoms as we only wore loin cloths. If it was too hot in the summer months the school was shut for the holidays, and if it rained we dispersed again. We had a red-faced teacher called Shiv Singh. As you know, Lord Shiva is the most revered of the Hindu Gods, and as our teacher was a Sikh, having a name with such doctrinaire differences did not worry him. He was a barber by caste – another contradiction for a Sikh who believes in the sanctity of long hair. He was fairly good and methodical as a teacher while very free with the cane. He taught us to read and write in Urdu, also basic arithmetic and simple sums. When I was twelve my mother made a shirt for me. It was made of coarse, hand-made cloth, and the seams hurt me. I also started wearing long Indian pyjamas. I was enrolled at a school six miles away. Here you could stay for three years and finish middle school, and that was the limit for higher education. I remember I used to carry my shirt and pyjamas in a bundle and put them on when I approached the school. My shoes were made by the village cobbler. They were hard, pinched and blistered my feet. I had to soak them in mustard oil every night so that they would become pliable, and I could wear them with comfort, but they never did. I used to be tough in those days. I got up at sunrise and ran to school, six and a half miles away, in about an hour. There were other Brahmin boys at school: there were Raghu, Bishnu, Telu and Tilok and we all went together. We picked berries on the way for our mothers to pickle; we also picked and carried back heaps of wild weeds and edible plants for our mothers to make into vegetable curries and stews.

In all those years I never saw the face of a paisa. You did not need it. All the necessary comforts were provided and there were no sweet shops where you could spend your money. Our only delicacy in those days was a lump of gur which was chewed on with great contentment and appreciation. A man did not need much in those days. Things were cheap and plentiful, so the goods you had in plenty you took to a neighbour, exchanging them for the goods they had in plenty. Sometimes I stayed with my aunt at nights and read her the *Gita* for a meal and a bed. The only discomfort in her house was that it was full of rats. She, being a widow, did not patch her walls and the rats came from the houses behind hers. Her house was a mud house with three rooms in it, and every rainy season it collapsed. It was then that all three of us brothers went to her aid and built it up again until the next rainy season. All her charpoys used to get soaked and her wooden trunks and boxes were all covered with water marks. She did not own many worldly goods, or money, but she always had plenty of food. People in the village held her in respect. She was a Brahmin widow, so she had everything given to her. She maintained that she was not living on charity but it was her right being a Brahmin widow. Anyway, people gave to her in the hope that they would be forgiven by God for their sins, but all their gifts weighed on her soul. She took vast quantities of snuff, and as soon as you neared her house you were sure to have a fit of sneezing. She was very headstrong and stubborn and always did as she wished. You just had to accept her, read her the *Gita* and go to sleep. That was Aunt Bhago. I had another one in the same street called Lajo. These were the only two sisters my mother had and she was the eldest. Lajo was not well liked by my mother. She was married to a priest called Kheru. Uncle Kheru made a good living out of conducting marriages, naming ceremonies and prayers for the dead and the new-born. His wife was credulous and suspicious. She had a habit of wandering the streets and looked simple. She often complained that my mother, being the oldest, took all the luck and family wits, which to some extent was true. Aunt Lajo had a son of my age and an older daughter. The daughter was married and never had a child, and the son had two sons, one club-footed and one epileptic. Then the son was declared lost in Burmah during the Second World War, and never came back. This broke Aunt Lajo's heart. She grew emaciated and wrinkled, so during her last few years she looked like a wizened monkey, and injured herself by biting herself and pulling her own hair. It is good that she died some time ago.

To come back to my story, I left Rurkala School at the age of fourteen and went to the Mission School at Salandhore. I stayed in a ramshackle boarding house and came home at weekends. The Mission School had English teachers and the discipline was strict. I was very bewildered at first by their way of life: eating with knives and forks which I had never practised. The only implement I had was given by nature – my fingers, which never failed me. The other boys tittered and laughed while I practised my new tricks with the knife and the fork. In the end I gave up and took all my meals in my room. I walked twelve to fourteen miles on Friday nights and left early Sunday mornings to come back. It made me cry to leave home, and I cried all the way up to the river. Here I stopped, washed my feet and my face ritualistically, then put on a brave face for the rest of the journey. Nowadays, young people are too soft and ease-loving, taking the luxuries of bikes and trains for granted. But we did not taste them in our day and did not know any better. This was the time I started smoking. I blame my father for this bad habit. He believed that smoking was the correct culmination of youth. So he started me on his Hukkah, and I curse him for that. He was a lazy, bone idle fellow; the only effort he made was to be born and then he had no choice; he wasted his money and died. His life was meaningless, aimless and wasteful like the rest of them. He sat in the same spot day after day playing cards and relishing any gossip that came his way.

After I had passed the Matriculation examination, I was called back. Here I stayed doing nothing like most other young men, and waiting for opportunity to open its doors. But the jobs were even scarcer then and I anticipated that I would spend the rest of my life tending a cow or two, playing cards, watching the years pass by and eventually becoming an old man and dying. This was the time when they married me off. I had no job and I did not know what marriage entailed, but nevertheless I was led into it to be slaughtered at the ritualistic altar. Of course, when men become slaves to tradition rather than enslaving the tradition, the system becomes a horrible cruelty, and men grow weak and fatalistic and dare not shake it off. So it was then and still is. I was married to a mere child seven years younger than I was, who did not know how to write her name, who was stubborn, dogmatic and credulous. I have tried to make the best of a blunder made by my parents on my behalf. But if I had to live all over again I would refuse to do so. Things could have been better for all of us. Yet it took me a long time to understand her and to accept her limitations. Your mother has her good points, she is kind, gentle, honest and truthful, but most of all loving to all of us.

While I was spending my days in those times waiting for something to turn up, I saw a post advertised for a junior teacher at my old school at Rurkala. I applied for it and another boy who was idle like me did the same. His name was Raghu. We knew each other's secrets but pretended we did not know each other when we met. When I look back now it seems funny, but in those days we kept an eye on each other and sniffed for any information and clues about what was happening without ever asking a direct question. Anyway, I was lucky and got the job and Raghu was left to wander about for another two years. But now he is much better off than I am working as a senior government officer in New Delhi. He will have a big government pension and a house to retire to. I sometimes wonder what would have happened to me if I had not got that job. You see, I never planned a thing in my life but let events happen to me. I never knew that I would like to be a teacher. I could so easily have been a clerk, an accountant, or a cashier, or a surveyor, and perhaps been equally content with life? Most of the people lived like that and still do. But this was the end of parental responsibility for me. I was married, had a job and could start life on my own. I got fifteen rupees a month, gave ten of it to my mother and kept five. For three long years I walked the same dusty roads in winter, summer and in the rainy seasons.

Then, one day, I happened to be glancing at a newspaper and saw some award schemes for people intending to train as teachers. I applied for one and was successful. After leaving your mother with my mother I went away to Multan. I had a suitcase, a basket of sweets and some fruit. The train was crowded and it was very hot. I must have dozed for a few minutes but when I woke up the basket and the suitcase were gone. Luckily, I had some money sewn in my inner pocket by your clever mother – that saved me. I had no change of clothes for six months. I remember having to wash my clothes at night, reading by a dim, kerosene lamp with doors bolted in case anyone should spot my nakedness! Yes, it was a hard struggle for survival but I managed to win the battle. The Principal of the Training College was an English man called John Hood, B.A. Oxon., M.A. He used to chew at a pipe continually, and was a cheerful, red-faced man. He used to teach principles of education, and my pronunciation of English was poor being a self-taught man. One day while preparing a lesson in his presence I mispronounced the word 'huge' as 'hug', and he just could not stop laughing. Then he started calling me Mr Hug; it was very embarrassing for me but I have never forgotten the episode or the laughter. After qualifying as a trained teacher I moved away from home to a high school since my status had gone up. Here I stayed for twenty-two years at Leelapore. That was your birthplace. You were all born there. And from a junior teacher I became the deputy head. I was then the father of four children. But I did not waste time, which is why I often say that I am a self-made man. Life was hard for me. I had a job with very large classes, sometimes over fifty youths in each, a noisy family and heaps of marking to do. Night after night I shut myself in a lonely bare room and studied for a degree and successfully obtained one. At forty, I was still working hard for a higher degree and did my bachelor of teaching. Yes, whenever opportunity came I grabbed it even against the odds. I don't know if I could have done better in another field. One cannot say. But I have taught scores, hundreds, of illiterate boys and some girls. I tried, with humility, to teach them to appreciate poetry, drama and other forms of literature in other languages. I taught them mathematics, history and geography. I have tried to make them imaginative and visionary; to show that there are other places beside their own; to understand and appreciate their own home, before they learn to appreciate other places. I taught them ancient Vedic history. In its classical, original context, devoid of all myth and dogma, it is the best in the world. If I have been able to enlighten some people and do away with illiteracy the tiniest bit, I think my life has been useful. I have always taken on women to coach privately as it is an all-boys' school. Some of them have been unhappily married; some of them were bright and lacked opportunity. I have taught them without taking money and have got them all through their matriculation. This must make some difference to their lives.

After serving for two decades and two years, I moved once again to my old school at Rurkala, this time as head of the school. By now the building was in ruins and the place had an aura of failure stamped all over it. When I first went to view it after a long absence it was all overgrown with scrub and prickly thorn bushes, with goatherds using the grounds for grazing. It was in the middle of a ruined Muslim burial ground and the boys played with the old skulls for footballs. I put a stop to it all, made them collect all the bones and had them reburied in consecrated ground. I have worked hard and made it into a high school – one of the best in the district. I have travelled at dawn from village to village to raise funds for buildings, books and equipment and I have partially succeeded. The school has now flowerbeds and orchards instead of scrub. It has modern, airy buildings. Where there were burial grounds once, there are playing fields, and the school has a big library. I have lived to see a dream come true and I think my life has not been in vain. So here is a moral for you. Always strive for something better and useful in your lives.

THE STRANGE TALE OF THE GAMA FAMILY

'Vijay, you old bastard, come and sit on my knee. Whose son are you?'

'My mother's.'

'Here is a smack for your bottom and no sweet today!'

'Yours!'

'Come on my darling, little son of a monkey. And you, little girl, what are you staring at, all owl-eyed at me? Haven't you seen me before? Your old uncle Pura.' The old man with a snow-white beard, all pointed and hair to match, looked like Santa Claus. His face was red, his eyes were yellow and he beat red-hot iron on an anvil with a hammer all day. He sat on a stool before a furnace, a furnace that hissed and sang, and many a time he let me turn the handle to churn the air and blow into the furnace. His coarse shirt was always wet with rivers of sweat. So wet that he used to wring it and let the sweat trickle down in a little salty stream. The old man had a big soft pouch of a belly and he liked to play with children. Vijay was his favourite.

Pura had a son called Gama and a daughter called Gamee. They were both tall, fair and pink. Gama did not like Gamee, so they often

87

had fights with fists and slaps, and in the end Gamee cried for a very long time. The old man's wife loved Gamee but did not like Gama much. The old woman walked stoopingly and looked like a witch. She propelled herself with a mulberry stick. Her wrinkled forehead was vast and protruding; her eyes looked like sunken wells with distant, deep, shimmering waters, and she sighed and talked to herself as she went walking and muttering with the mulberry stick. People said that she knew magic, that at night she turned into a goat and roamed around the village. Vijay and Asha feared the old lady but loved the old man. The old woman was said to have given birth to thirteen sons but they all died. In the end she persuaded Pura to remarry. He had two children, but his second wife died in childbirth, and Gama was fostered and fed by the wife of a poor cobbler, and in order that no evil eye might harm him he was named after a beggar.

People speculated that foul play was involved in the death of Gama's mother. They alleged that the Old Witch got her with her evil magic because she wanted to possess the two children. The Old Witch also had a brother who was chronically sick. Gamee often told stories about his illness. 'He shot at the horse of Sain Das.' Sain Das was said to be the original inhabitant of the village and had laid its first foundation stone. His spirit now guards the village and rides a black spirit horse. 'My uncle was aiming at a tree and all of a sudden Sain Das appeared on his horse. His horse got shot by accident and was rendered blind.' But Sain Das's spirit is an unforgiving spirit, and although the horse was shot in the eye by pure accident he made the uncle suffer for it. After a long, agonising illness when the young man twisted and turned, writhed in agony, begged forgiveness from Sain Das for his sins to no avail, he died raving mad, twitching, foaming and screaming. People again blamed the sister; they said that she could have done something to save her brother's life for did she not know the art of curing sore eyes? She could have interceded with the Saint and healed his horse's eye. The old lady, indeed, possessed a healing touch which cured a lot of undiagnosed eye ailments. Once, on fireworks night, Vijay injured his eye with a rocket which went off in his hand. His eye was burnt and damaged and he was taken twice daily to the old woman's house which was at the end of a narrow, high alley. The old woman muttered a long incantation and then blew on Vijay's eye twice at the end of the recitation. And Vijay's eye was miraculously healed after a few days.

When Gamee grew up into a young woman she became unusually pretty. She had very well-developed breasts and 'eyes that could talk', so the village women said. She, too, was attributed a bad reputation with young men. She winked winsomely at some idle young men, as I often observed, and smiled. She even used her eyes to relate long messages, when talking between boys and girls was strictly prohibited. She also had a habit of swaying her hips both ways as she walked. Gamee was never allowed to dress up or wear pretty clothes. Her clothes were always dirty, patched and shabby. She cursed the old woman under her breath for never allowing her to wear anything attractive. If she had a nice white kameez (shirt), the old woman would dust a piece of furniture with it before allowing her to wear it. She had a belief that dusty clothes protected Gamee. Gamee was not even allowed to wash her face and hands with soap as it was scented. So Gamee always brought a piece of stolen soap to the smithy, carefully tucked away in her pocket, and spent hours scrubbing and lathering her face and hands repeatedly under our tap. She also spent a long time making ringlets out of her hair, but when it was time to go home she messed her hair and smudged her face again, and she even rubbed some cow dung on the end of her nose to take away the smell of scent. She always walked away from the workshop, arrogantly swinging her hips and gently balancing a basket of dung-cakes piled up high on her head. She never needed to touch the basket with her hands so elegantly had she mastered the art of balancing.

Gamee liked to eat lemons and she ate them by the score, raw. She said that lemons made her lips red and juicy. She often raided the nearby fields in search of ripe lemons and took Asha along with her. One day Asha found her hiding behind a huge cacti bush with a big man who was kissing and smothering her and making strange grunts and moans in his throat while Gamee kept giggling and wanted to run away. Asha rushed to her aid but Gamee told her to go away. She gave her all the lemons and told her not to tell anyone about the man. But Asha was concerned, he could have killed her, and she wondered at the strangeness of grown-ups. Then one day

Gamee was married off to an ugly, very dark, spotty-faced man, and never came to the smithy again.

Gama and Gamee were never sent to school so they did not know how to read and write. But Gama was a very strong man and being unable to read did not worry him. He had very large hands and fat arms; if he caught Asha's arm with one hand the arm would go all bloodless, white and dead, while she would squirm under his grip. Gama had ugly hands covered in warts and he always wore a pink turban. He never tied it neatly so it just hung around his neck in loops, looking more like an upturned bamboo basket. He was musical and used to play tunes on an upturned bucket. The tunes he liked were popular film songs from the city which he played deftly on the bucket with his stubby, fat fingers. Gama looked like his sister. He also had big breasts but he never covered them up, so they looked wobbly and funny on him. Gama had grown a moustache. A beard had started to sprout on his face. So at the age of fifteen he pretended he was grown up. He kept the company of young men who hung about where the women gathered. He listened to their talk with a half-smiling roguish grin. Gama's method of impressing a young woman was to show his body with the least amount of clothing and strut about in the briefest of shorts. He usually did odd jobs for people who had grown-up daughters, without charging them, and was very happy to run errands and whistle about all day. He did not help his old father in the smithy. The father used to pursue Gama, calling him abusive names, 'you son of a donkey', 'you son of an owl', 'you mother fucker', and so on and so forth. But Gama generally pleased himself, roaming the streets in the company of undesirable people and those of dubious reputation. His mother cursed and cried, his father called him wicked and perverse but Gama, being the only son, grinned and was out of the house like a dart.

One day Gama's father did not sit at the anvil. Instead he sat on a chair and sighed. When people asked what was wrong, he did not answer. But to Asha and Vijay he told a story. A story of the vision he had seen on his death bed.

'It may be thirty years or more ago when once I fell ill, and was poorly for a very long time. I was a young man then and very fit. I grew thin and lay on my bed waiting for the God of Death – Yama –

to call and then one day I saw him. He was big and black, strong and giant-like, and he stood there at the foot of my bed motioning with his long finger to follow him. I was terrified but I followed him. For a long time we flew in the sky, and I saw streets with blue and yellow houses. I saw all varieties of sweetmeats littered all around and I wanted one badly and bent down to pick one. But Yama did not like it; he kicked me in the small of my back. Then he came to a vast house made with luminous gold bricks studded with diamonds, and all around the house stood guards. I stood outside while Yama went in. He came out and told me to follow him again. This time, I followed at a distance through unending, narrow alleyways all brightly lit with chandeliers. Then we came into a massive, airy and spacious hall hung with tassels with cloth of gold. There sat an elderly, benign, kind old man. He had a long white beard and round glasses rested at the tip of his nose. He examined me slowly from head to toe, then looked in a huge book and read all the records of my deeds. Suddenly he stopped and his face turned pale, and he motioned the Death God Yama to him. He said, "I reckon you made a mistake once again. This man is not the man who is destined to end. His life has some time to run yet."

'Yama was very apologetic and he stared back on his journey with me. The next thing I remember I had regained consciousness. When I looked around I was laid out in the crematorium under a pile of wood, and ready to be set alight. However, I was brought back home, and the very same day Pura the Carpenter died. They must have mistaken me for him. You see even God can make mistakes. But before Yama left he told me in the strictest terms not ever to mention the visions I saw. But human nature is frail and I for one cannot keep a secret. I know I shall suffer for my disobedience. Last night, I saw the same Yama again and I know my end is near.'

The old man looked shrunken and tearful. His hands were trembling a little as he tried to keep his tears back. Within a month he was dead. So now Gama attained his full freedom. He misspent most of his father's wealth and his own time in gambling and drink. He also entertained the village vagabonds and layabouts in his workshop and often acted as a go-between for the foolish young girls and many rascals.

'Gama, Oh Gama. Where are you my Moon, my Son?'

'Shut up you old bitch. Go back to your cooking.'

'Son, keep away from Sohna, he will ruin you, I pray.'

'Mind your own business, you bloody bitch, I know what's good for me. Buzz off now, or I will crack your pot-head in two.' The old woman ran scuttling like a hen, and as she ran she wiped the tears from her eyes with the corner of her Duppatta. She saw Asha perched as usual, cross-legged on the top of her courtyard wall observing everything with half-shut eyes, like a cat in the sun. The humiliated old woman tried to smile, but her smile was contrived and embarrassed. Gama sat in the winter sun sprawled in any easy chair which his father had made for himself. He continued to snarl and grumble then shut his eyes. Gama grew three nipples on his ample breasts, and as he lay without a shirt Asha remembered the boast he made the other day about being equivalent to one and a half men.

The early sun was warm and it made Asha lazy, and she dozed a little. Then she saw Gama light a match and throw it on his buffalo. The buffalo's hairy coat was full of lice. Gama used to ride the buffalo and was similarly infested. And now he had sought out a quick solution. He went on deftly burning the hair and wiping the buffalo's skin with a damp cloth. The buffalo was apparently in pain, and she kicked Gama, and he lay sprawled out in dung and mud. There was a muffled titter while Gama shouted and scowled at the girl, 'You wait till you grow up. I shall get even with you, you little monkey!' Jito came out of the house, giggling as usual, and asking what was wrong. But Asha did not answer so she went in with her big buttocks swaying and huge breasts dangling. Presently Gama came out and went into Jito's house. Asha's mother called, 'Come down, you little dare devil. You are not a child anymore. I wonder what people will say, seeing you monkeying about like that! Have some womanly shame and cover your head.'

'It is hot mother and my hair is long and fine. I shall not wear a duppatta simply because you ask me to.'

'How dare you ask questions, answer back and argue? She is bad through and through. That's what comes out of education! Dear God, I'd never have dreamt, at her age, to answer back and not cover my head. At her age I was a married woman. The Iron Age is here for sure, that's the long and short of it. I am afraid for that girl. The others are modest and shy and have all the womanly virtues but Asha is impudent. I wonder what she will bring to our name when she grows up? Our family has never been talked about in three generations. The trouble is she is already too conscious of her looks. I have often observed her looking at her clothes and then smiling to herself. Well, these are very bad signs for a young girl! She pays too much attention to her body, and then she looks at you with mischievous eyes, and she laughs too fully and too loudly.' Then kindness shows and mother says, 'However, she is still a child yet. I am prepared to forgive. But I would rather see a daughter of mine perish than bring shame upon the household. It is all her father's fault. I told him not to send her to school but would he listen? Asha, come on down this instant, Asha come on down quick.'

Asha felt guilty, came down and put her duppatta on dutifully and tried to repeat the instructions like an incantation in order not to forget. 'I must not walk with my shoulders held high. I must not look at faces but stare at the floor. I must not look at my clothes and admire myself. I must not smile to myself. I must not ask for new clothes any more.'

Buddha, the village sweeper as she was known, was a legendary character like Gama. She was thin – a little woman with a wrinkled, monkey-like face and dirty grey hair. Her little eyes were like slits and they always had a yellow film over them. She screwed them up tight when talking to people, so it appeared as if she had difficulty in seeing. She had come to the village as a bride some fifty years back. Some people who still recall her from those days say that she was the prettiest little girl in her red Shalwar, and she told so many jokes as she went around that every woman wanted her to sweep for her.

Buddha soon got most of the houses to clean as she was a good entertainer and did not complain if she had to do extra work. People say that in those days she always had a smile on her face instead of that grimness and sullenness which later took its place. She was

fairly well off with the generous quantity of food she got instead of
wages; she also got plenty of clothes to wear which the women
discarded. She had two little daughters who soon grew up to assist
their mother. They carried her rubbish baskets and brushes and
helped to make dung-cakes with her. Time went on, the girls grew
into young women and were married off and left the village. Then
Buddha's husband died of appendicitis. Buddha said it was a terrible
pain in his side which must have been witchcraft! Buddha was a
widow now and she wanted to leave the village. But people were
good to her, and Balik Singh personally went to her and assured her
that her interests would be safe. The sweeper woman stayed on.
Then, one day, she did not turn up for work. People called at her
ramshackle hut to see if she was unwell. But she just seemed to have
vanished. Balik Singh and others soon took possession of her
meagre belongings including her little hut which they used for
butchering goats in privacy. But the condition of the village
deteriorated. The drains were all blocked up and the streets were full
to overflowing with goat-droppings and children's excrement. The
whole village stank and people started falling ill.

Then, very mysteriously, Buddha turned up again. People tried to
question her but she kept strict silence. But, somehow, the story
behind her flight leaked out and is still remembered and retold, with
innuendoes and relish. 'It was that sweeper fellow. The one who
used to visit her. He was from Nuala. He was that fair chap. Don't
you remember? The one she called her "cousin". Some cousin I
would say. Her son takes after him, he is his exact image. Well,
Buddha got pulled to him. Being a widow and a woman she left the
security of her house for that fellow. Why, I knew before that this
would happen. You remember, I told you? I said, I tell you that
woman is not in her senses anymore. She would follow that monkey
of a man, that ass!' And she did.

She took all her gold jewellery, the money and went to live with
him.

'That is what she does, the silly woman. That's how she repays us
all for our kindness! Why, sometimes I used to give her two
chapattis for cleaning up that little patch which I could have done
myself seven times over. I always gave her curries – a generous

amount of them. You know, some people, they give the sweeper stale chapattis buttered with oil or just dry or lighter than their own and never give any vegetables. But I never did that. I always thought she was one of us. But not anymore. She has brought shame upon us all. I wouldn't go near her, even if she was dying. She should have realised what she was doing and letting herself in for. She had a family and knew what men were like but some women are like her. Even when they are widowed they lust after men and have strong animal passions. You know the story of the man who married someone just like her and could not satisfy her. She wanted more and more and then one day he got so fed up that he pushed a stick up her. Well, I can understand that. Some women have no shame.'

The talk went on and on and everyone in the street had their own pet version of the story. But Buddha was a remarkable woman. Being a menial she could not retaliate. The only way forward for her was to keep quiet, and bear all the gossip and malicious talk. It was true that the woman was enticed by a neighbouring married sweeper who, after taking all her money, wished to sell her to another sweeper. Buddha learnt about the plot just in time to run away. Later on she had a son who was very handsome but grew up to be a frustrated and violent young man. To add to his frustrations, he had a speech defect and was mentally subnormal. Anyhow, Buddha arranged his marriage but the bride, finding her husband simple, left him, taking all Buddha's savings and jewellery the second time around. Buddha was once again a pauper with the burden of a retarded son. Gama often set the boy against his mother. The boy was easily led and was very emotional for his age; he also believed everything that he was told. If someone said, 'Your mother was visited by five men last night, is a common prostitute, aren't you ashamed of her? You ought to do something about your honour,' he would rush home and start beating his mother, ruin her belongings and break all her pots and pans. So Buddha the underling had a miserable and tragic life, and she fervently hoped that in her future life her sins would be forgiven and God would end her further cycles of birth.

After Buddha's sad exit the street grew quiet once more till Sēman the waterman's son came whistling and singing a film tune through his teeth. Jito peeped out again, remarking, 'That boy needs his head examined.' She winked and went in again. Sēman was pleased to be noticed. Now on his face he wore a fat grin. Then he stopped in front of Gama's workshop. Gama came to the doorstep and Sēman joined him. They sat in front of an empty, upturned tin bucket. Sēman started to sing, his head up in the air like a braying donkey while Gama beat the rhythm. Sēman was another of the village idlers. He was fairly bright at school, but his mother could not afford the fees, besides he helped her to carry the full pitchers and also fill them with water from the well. He had two notorious elder sisters. The younger one was reputed to be 'faster' than the older one. She received a lot of fanmail from young men, but being illiterate herself, she often sought Asha's help to read and write to them for her. She stored these letters in her bra. She also had an ugly admirer from the army. Once Asha saw him madly waving a red silk scarf so she took to her heels. To Asha he looked sinister and criminal. There were some ruined houses next to her house and he kept pacing through them, up and down, down and up, then he turned back and watched until Sēman's sister came out. Asha's curiosity could not be restrained, she put her eye to the chink in the wall – the girl lay naked, writhing on the dirty, dusty floor as the man was biting her. Asha was too scared to keep on looking in case he committed a murder so she yelled and ran away, thus disturbing the amorous lovers. Sēman, like his sisters, was idle and wandered about the village to while away the heavy hours. He associated with petty thieves and vandalised people's property. Asha's father had erected a fence around his fields to keep the stray cattle and humans out of them – it was a novel idea. This was a new challenge to Sēman and his friends: they tried their strength in the moonlit nights, ripping all the fence up, toppling all the massive brick columns which supported the barbed wire. The village council was too preoccupied – or too timid – to take note of vandalism. These lads marched in groups with arms linked to show their solidarity and strength. Sometimes, if they saw a girl alone, they blocked her path and bullied her. They had another member of the gang – a Brahmin boy. His name was Shri. He had an aged father who had a grocer's shop but never did much trade. He was now blind and helpless but Shri's mother, being a Brahmin, got enough charity to subsist. Shri took to gambling and drinking. He stopped going to school and spent most of his time at Gama's workshop. He was fond of bragging and reading poetry aloud, often boasting of having composed it. He would laboriously copy poems in a red book and add a few additional lines. He always had lots of schemes for making easy money but never put them into practice. All these young men with time on their hands roamed the streets nonstop day and night. Their ways of amusing themselves were severely limited: they chased stray dogs, and had cock fights. To glamorise their lives they created myths and fantasies, conjuring up visions of adventure and great wealth as they lived from day to day. What they lacked in reality they made up with imagination.

At twelve each day Asha went to the post office to fetch mail while Vijay was away at boarding school. She was in the habit of skipping and running. So she would skip and run. She would pass the big pond and pause before a huge stone in one corner. It was a large millstone but was used as a seat for people to sit on. If it was unoccupied Asha would sit a minute and then run again. She would pause before a derelict, one-roomed workshop which had a brightly coloured map painted on the wall. The workshop belonged to a tailor who had long since vacated it; now only bats lodged there. The tailor had eloped with a girl from the village. People said that if he ever returned they would kill him. He had a very sullen looking, cruel son who was a member of the Gama group, and sometimes all of them congregated in the gloom indulging in strange practices. Asha's mother had told her not to look inside that room but this made Asha look all the more. It was a dark room with piles of straw on the floor. There was no other furniture in it except the garish map which stared at one. Asha would trot again, circling around the farmers' homes. There was a row of half a dozen houses which belonged to one family. As they multiplied they occupied more and more of the street. The women in these houses were always shabbily dressed, with an air of fatalistic gloom and resignation about them. They had long, uncombed hair and shabby duppattas. These were subsistence peasants making hardly enough to live on. But they seemed to have endless numbers of half-dressed children. Their heights ranged from three feet to about eight inches, there being a difference of an inch or so between each child. Asha, being a Brahmin girl, had the terrible misfortune of visiting these houses on certain auspicious occasions. For example, on the God Serpent Day she was invited to bless the house, and was the first to be fed on thick, homemade pasta before the family could break the fast. They rolled the pasta in single strands using upturned pitchers and their hands which they used as rolling pins and when sufficient length of pasta was rolled they hung strings of it across the lines to dry. After the whole process the pasta looked like fat, grey earthworms. The women stewed cauldrons of it in molasses, and on the day Asha was the first to taste it. They would prepare their one-roomed mud houses with a fresh coat of dung and red ochre, and then scrub all the piles of sky-high pots and pans, tumblers, jugs, plates till the dim, unlit room glistened with the glow from rows of brass pots. They would proudly escort Asha to the room. An elderly woman would proceed to wash her feet, tie the red, sacred thread on her left arm, and mark her forehead with red vermilion and sandalwood paste. Then she was given a clean mat to sit on and was served with a plateful of these pasta earthworms. This was the most difficult part of the ritual where she had to swallow them. After she had gingerly wrapped them around her fingers she would dare to push them in her mouth. They were like pieces of swollen rubber bands which took a lot of chewing and would not descend down the gullet. Seeing that she took such a long time the housewife would become impatient since she had the whole family waiting to be fed. So she would take a paisa which was tied at one end of her shawl and give it to her as her due for coming, and tell her to eat the rest at home. And that was the grand escape for Asha – a thing she dearly wished to do. She would gallop homewards and give the syrupy mess to the cow who licked up every bit of it. Asha would run to the shop clutching her paisa and spend it on boiled sweets, tamarind, dried berries or a balloon. On the whole these were quiet people, they never asked Asha any questions and were religious and God-fearing.

Then she reached one-eyed Chinty's house. Now she was a real busybody, exceedingly curious about all the village gossip, rumours, stories. She seemed to chew at these with her yellowed teeth, her tongue salivated, she licked her lips and all the time her one good eye went up and down rapidly in her forehead. People hated her and loathed her habits of spiteful tale-bearing. She had one of those brazen faces which look agelessly menancing. She had a long, hook nose and looked to Asha like a cunning owl. She always had a cynical smile on her face and a tested method of pumping out information. Seeing Asha from a distance she would stop spinning and shout, 'Hi, there! That's the sweet little girl I was waiting for. You look tired, come and have a rest.' She would point to the empty space on the doorstep, and after the girl had seated herself down Chinty would carefully look her up and down to see how much she had grown since yesterday, and then say with a sweet giggle, 'Well, I never knew you had grown up. My, you are a big girl now. Soon your father will have to find a boy.' Hearing this, Asha's face would turn crimson with embarrassment and she would protest, 'I don't want a "boy". I don't ever want to get married!' Chinty would become philosophical and mutter, 'No matter how much book learning you do, in the end you have to get married and have little children. This is the Lord's rule. This is how it has been always. Even you must have a man.' Then she would give a short giggle and her eye would critically rest on Asha's nubile bosom making its presence known through her thin muslin frock and say again, 'My, you have grown, how you have grown!' It was Chinty's business to keep a mental note of all the grown-up and growing girls and note their activities and bearings and she was usually the source of all scandal. The kind of preliminary talk with Asha followed as a prelude to something more weighty, and she would begin. 'By the way, I don't want to be nosy but who were all those men I heard talking, coming out from your first floor? Is Malika home then?'

'No, it must have been our radio.'

'No, I am certain it was not. I can tell when the machine talks. No, there's no mistaking, they were human, men's voices. Maybe it was that young fellow that often goes to your house. What's his name again? Well, it is nothing to be ashamed of. We've all got friends.' And she would look up questioningly with an expectant look in her one eye. Asha would get up ready to go and Chinty would shout, 'See if there's a letter for Aunt Chinty? Though I am not so hopeful. Nobody writes to me. It must be nice to get letters. You get a lot of them, don't you? You must have some nice friends.' She would go on talking softly and Asha did not always understand her double meanings, hints and innuendoes. Then she would go past Shri's father's shop. The blind man sat immobile as usual on an empty corn sack which, due to the many holes in it, was now serving as a mat. His big paunch had the sacred thread crossing it and he kept off flies with the rhythmic swing of the corner of his dhoti (loin cloth). Asha would stop to chat with him for a second and then trot off again. Then she would come to Meeto's house and avert her gaze as she passed. Meeto was a carpenter's daughter who drank heavily and who, they say, squandered all her father's money on drink. The family had a little house in the Bazaar. To have a house in the Bazaar was a very uncultured and brazen thing to do but to have a whorehouse was the limit! Meeto ran this house. She was a squat, ugly girl with city manners. So every woman hated her as much as men adored her. They often turned around to have a second look at her and wolf-whistled at her. All this attention was mildly interesting to Meeto and she would smile graciously and chirp out, 'You naughty one, you so and so, you would never learn. I could teach you a thing or two. I have a few minutes at ten tonight, if you care.'

Then there was the sissy blacksmith's workshop. He imitated all the ways of women including walking, talking and working. He was a much laughed at, harmless, middle-aged bachelor who led a quiet, eventless life. Her uncle's shop, as usual, was filled with men including Balik Singh in his snow-white clothes. Her uncle would read the paper aloud to them or sometimes just play cards or chess, or just chat. Under the banyan tree in the square, tethered to its ancient roots, a cow or two would be staring, a couple of farmers would be chatting, or a group of boys would be noisily playing shatranj. Then the world of the post office would loom up. The post office world contained a large number of sweaty youths with strong-smelling clothes but very well-combed hair. This was the world of urgency and expectation. The post office building was a one-roomed mud hut in the Bazaar. Outside on the wall hung the symbol of the post office in the shape of a dingy little red box – the only one of its kind in the whole village. The postmaster was the only employee of this domain. He performed the duties of a sorter of letters, postal and money orders and occasionally parcels. He was also supposed to deliver the mail. He was related to Asha in a convoluted kinship manner, and she called him 'grandfather'. He was a very dark, small man with sore, red eyes and always spoke in a hoarse voice, and it seemed as if at any minute he would choke and stifle. Asha could imitate his voice perfectly and was much praised at home for this mimicry. Though he only got a small salary from the post office he was fairly well off. Being a Brahmin priest he owned some ancestral clients who on auspicious days gave him a great deal of food and sweetmeats. A granddaughter of his, like other Brahmin girls in the village, went from door to door to the appointed houses, blessed them and collected rations of flour, sugar, butter and chapattis. But Asha's father condemned this ritual as mere begging and stipulated that no daughter of his would set foot out of the house with a tray, so his share of families was ungratefully divided among the Brahmin clan. The postmaster was named after the Goddess Kali but Asha always called him 'Kala Haran' meaning black deer. This was an appropriate name for him – he was very black, always walked on foot, had sore eyes, a pointed face and did resemble an old buck. He always got free fodder for his cows for rendering postal services to ignorant farmers. They respected him and feared his wisdom for who else could bring them letters and money from such faraway places as Australia, Canada and England? So they never forgot to give Kala Haran a small share of their good fortune.

Kala Haran had no chair or desk in his little room. He squatted on an old hessian mat and used an upturned box for his letters and his stamp pad rested on it. If an auditor happened to come and check affairs, he would borrow a chair and a battered desk from Asha's uncle and seat him under the shade of a banyan tree, and would run back and forth like a deer with red files under his arm. But it was the same auditor year after year whose visits and face became quite familiar to the people. These were the only days when Kala Haran was very strict, not allowing anyone to enter his hut, but the rest of the time his doors were open to all and sundry – the more the merrier. Come winter, come summer, his little hut used to be full to overflowing with young idlers from all corners of the village. This was their most frequented meeting place and here they could play cards, crack smutty jokes, freely savour rumours and, very importantly also, keep an eye on who got a letter and from where.

At the stroke of twelve noon Kala Haran would leave his house to wander slowly off to the post office. By the time he drew nearer to the premises a crowd would already have gathered like a swarm of bees. Kala Haran would take a key out of his pocket most delicately and undo the lock which hung at the end of a chain like a large amulet. As soon as he opened the door there would be one great mad rush as the youths would vie with each other to find a space to squat in. Those who did not push in time or were unlucky had to stand outside in the burning sun. Inside, they all squatted on the mud floor which was cool, and started whispering in the low voices of intrigue. They mostly wore short pants, and it seemed to Asha that their thighs, along with their unmentionable parts, would burst out any minute. The thought of this materialising made Asha fearful as she was the only girl present. Some of them were self-conscious and realising this eventuality kept pushing their shirt tails in front of them; others resented her presence and glared at her. But the majority of them could not care less and were very proud to display their physique; they oiled themselves and wore very little in the summer. There was Shri there, of course, Gama and Sēma and many of their pals. The majority of them never got a letter in their lives, and if they had, many would have found it difficult to decipher it, but all the same they went there with clockwork regularity. They kept a mental note of who got mail from where. Very often letters were lifted, especially the ones they suspected were love letters to village girls.

At one o'clock or thereafter, a perspiring little Sikh man would appear with a bag on his bike from the neighbouring sub-post office and after delivering his load would rush away. Now all the mob's attention would concentrate on the bag as if they were a pack of hounds and the postbag a rabbit. Some of them would rub their hands, licking their lips in anticipation, and would grow impatient at the slowness of Kala Haran who kept arranging and rearranging his dhoti. But in due course he undid the bag, started stamping the letters, postcards, envelopes, air letters, parcels, while the mob followed his every movement without ever missing a single detail. Their eyes would dart from the stamp to the stamped letter to the next one. Then the critical stage of calling out names would arrive – a complete stillness would pervade – and old Kala Haran's choking, hoarse voice would dully carry on, 'Amar Singh, Amrit Lal, Amrit Saria, Bakil Chand', and so on and at the roll call of each name many hands would extend saying, 'I will take that letter to Amar Singh', or Amrit Saria as the case may be. 'I go that way, he is my neighbour, or I have to call on him.' The old man would be only too glad to lighten his burden and save his shoes by parting with the mail at the doorstep, and most of it, somehow, got delivered this way. The youths, however, did not deliver the letters without reading them first. If they did not make a good job of resealing them they would tear them up and scatter the bits in the street. That was one of the reasons why Asha's father sent her daily to the post office to collect the newspaper and a few letters which would otherwise have often gone astray.

After this two-hour ordeal, she would be glad to come out in the open again and smell the dust and sunshine on the uneven footpath as she walked. She would decide to walk on the other side of the pavement so that she could evade nosy Chinty. She would pass Dr Kashmiri's surgery and see the fat doctor sprawled in an easy chair with his snow-white shirt and trousers on. She would pass Darshan's shop: as usual he would be combing his hair or killing the flies. She would automatically pause and search her pockets for any money she could spend. Sometimes she found a couple of paisas and went in. She wanted to look and sound natural and say, 'Can I have two paisa worth of sweets, Darshan?'

'Sorry, run out of sweets.'

'No, I don't want sweets, can I have a balloon?'

'No, no balloons either.'

'Well, I don't want to walk any further. Can you give me anything sweet? A piece of gur perhaps?' After having been served she took a short cut to the house by Saad Dacoit's house and was pleased to have come home. But she really enjoyed these journeys. She loved the freedom of all the roaming she was allowed to do, and running errands was no difficulty.

In the quickening dusk of winter nights Asha felt imprisoned in the big house and her soul ached to take wing and flee. She was lonely and isolated: of her destiny no one knew; of her thoughts she did not know herself. The little dusky oil lamps were lit, and they cast shadows like rings, and in these rings fluttered moths, prisoners of the little circles and whorls of light. Out of the brick house, mud houses and lowly huts silvery smoke emanated. It began as a fine streak and then assumed bulk, strength and shape. Sometimes it flew in small, acrid puffs resembling the soft, silky grey hair of a mermaid. Sometimes it came in such large masses that it looked like elephants riding skyward with their trunks pointing high, higher and then vanishing slowly and joining and mingling with the clouds in the distant horizon. It was the time when all the senses sharpened, the ears listened, listened in the stillness to the milking of a cow, listened to the bells, listened to the echoes of the eerie conch shells being blown at the temple and the gurdwaras when the mind's eye saw the fat priests blowing their cheeks out into puffballs till they almost burst and ached, putting life into dead shells so that they came alive, alive, so that one could sense the urgency and a sense of divinity all around, in the dark skies, in the houses and huts. In this urgency, even agnostics forgot their differences and uttered the word 'Om' and started praying. It was the time you heard the music of bullocks going homewards as their bells tinkled. This music was also sad and lonely as they trudged their weary way on the unmade roads, so you felt that their lives, although an endless burden, were useful too. With their big, dark eyes penetrating the curtain of darkness Asha felt that they felt and saw what she could not. In the fast falling dusk she saw the shapes of men and beasts like ghosts, visible yet undefined shadows. She saw the endless streams of donkeys as they came bowed down, carrying the last load of bricks for the day from the kiln as they passed by the pond. Some of them had bleeding necks and sore, scabby stomachs, and on the many lacerations lashed the stick and abuse of the carrier. Sometimes the donkeys could no longer carry their burdens, fell down, were mercilessly beaten in the chain of cruelty and gave up. It was at this time that Asha would feel most acutely the need to communicate and seek for herself amid human voices and human bodies. She found it pleasant to rub herself against her mother or a friend. This contact made her feel secure and her skin tingle with life. Seeing the night approach she would prepare for her daily visit to Gagari's, the waterman's house. The house was halfway between a mud hut and a brick house and stood looking dismal at the far end of the pond. It was a gloomy house which always looked ailing. As you reached it you could smell, strongly, the goats which were always tied in the compound. Sometimes there were baby goats which Asha liked to hug as they felt silk soft and warm. Compared to the aged, starving ugliness of their mothers they were alive and lively as they never sat still, frisked, frolicked and jumped about. Some of them were brown – brown with a red sheen, some of them were black – black with a black sheen, and some of them were dappled white-black, white-brown in triangles and squares. Their little tufty tails moved this way and that as they sang for their mothers 'ma, ma, ma' endlessly.

Gagari himself was a middle-aged man who had converted to Sikhism and had long hair and a turban. But his sons did not have turbans or belong to his religion. The family carried water in pitchers from the well for other villagers in the evenings and mornings but apart from that he also had a greengrocer's shop. So compared with other Jhir folk they were better off and proud of this fact. Gagari's wife never walked but crawled, creeping like a centipede. She seemed to have no life in her at all but every coming year she would produce a new child and up to now she had managed to collect eight daughters and two sons. These were the living children but it was assumed that quite a few of them had passed away in infancy. Her eldest son, who seemed to have a perpetual cold, assisted the father in his business. He had a constantly running nose and had got into the habit of breathing it in with a sucking noise after each word he uttered. After him there were four daughters and another son. Asha came to see the two older ones who were her friends. The elder girl was a quiet, wide-eyed, solemn, very dark girl who was also always ailing and catching numerous colds. But the younger one was lively, bouncy, energetic and vivacious who liked to dress up and sulked when her mother would not allow her to do so. She was always asking Asha for clothes she did not want and liked to dye her clothes in bright colours. She had a lighter skin than her sister but her features were not so sharp; she had a wide, round nose, rather deep-set eyes but her lips were always red and she had a good set of even, white teeth. She was a jolly girl who had a theory about her sister's colouring, maintaining that her pigment would get fairer as she became older. The elder sister was pretty and Asha wondered why the younger girl was always so concerned about her skin colour unless, of course, to cover her own plainness. Though the girls were illiterate, Asha preferred their company. She included another unhappy person in this trio – this was Jito's stepdaughter who was always overworked and half-starved. She was not allowed any time to play but all the same she joined in on odd occasions. Asha could only maintain this relationship without the knowledge of her family and visited them on the pretext of going for an evening walk.

After some time the older girl was married off and soon after died of TB. It appeared that half the family suffered from the disease including the younger son but they did not believe it and could not afford a cure, and all the ailing members were gladly left in God's good care. It was sad for Asha to see the little boy just lying in his bed crawling towards death like his sister. It was an unhealthy house, always exposed to the damp and fetid waters of the pond, and people in it were always sick and gloomy but nevertheless Asha liked to go there and spend her evenings with the goat and the girls.

I once saw a young woodpecker fledgling, sleek, fat and feathery, fly away from its nest, then the nest was not a nest anymore. I saw a petal fall from a rose but it was a rose no more. I saw a little girl grow up, and there was happiness no more.

The process of growing up was full of pain. All the freedom a girl had known in her childhood was snatched away from her at the advent of puberty, when most of the time of day she must spend indoors, behind the bamboo blinds till she is married, gratefully, to a man she has never seen. These restrictions were even more painfully enforced among the high classes. So when Asha was barely thirteen she, too, came to experience them. She could no longer talk to boys and between her and the opposite sex there was suddenly erected a high wall not of bricks and stones but made by the painful social arrangements. She must not look up, nor smile in public, she must not giggle, nor uncover her head. She must not talk loudly lest men should hear her and be attracted by her and, worst of all, she must not sit alone in case her thoughts wandered into prohibited territories. Asha was a solitary girl and enjoyed solitude. This sudden transition was hell. Suddenly she was made aware of the separateness of boys; before that she had not noticed the difference. It also made her stubborn, wilful and rebellious and she doggedly pursued the ends her mother labelled as wicked. She did not keep her eyes down as she walked, she laughed profusely and talked loudly, uncovering her hair and even took the duppatta up from her bosom as often as she could. But the saddest of all her experiences was that she could no longer understand her mother. There was a growing divide between them and their ways from henceforth were different. Her mother was painfully distressed by her wilfulness, her need to question her orders and love of flamboyant and colourful clothes, but her father said it was only a phase. To put her mother's mind at rest he removed her to the neighbouring village and enrolled her in his own all-boys school, under his watchful protection. This was a small town compared to the family's small village. Therefore, people of this town would never dream of marrying their daughters and sons to the small village's inhabitants. If they ever broke the rule it was done reluctantly and grudgingly and it was either because their daughters were past marriageable age or their sons had some physical defect such as lameness, general ugliness, were one-eyed, feeble-minded or had a stammer. The small village was called Sarē Marē while the large town was aptly named Sarē Dubē meaning 'all dead' and 'all drowned' respectively. The story was that both these towns in the ancient days had warring factions which attacked the outlying districts. Sarē Marē had killed all its foes and Sarē Dubē had drowned all its enemies in a freak flood. But these stories could not be checked for authenticity and the names were sometimes used to indicate the cowardice and spinelessness of the inhabitants. When a Sarē Marē daughter was lucky enough to be married to a Sarē Dubē son, she soon started being sarcastic about her own small village. She generally called it a 'pigsty' and put on city manners such as speaking in an affected voice, assuming a mincing walk, and starting to roll her eyes and raise her eyebrows when talking. These narrow prejudices were carried a step further, so much so that some Sarē Dubē citizens thought it a great insult to pass through Sarē Marē when going to the city. Now both these villages were a stone's throw from each other and the city was much nearer to Sarē Marē, yet these rich, prosperous people would never dream of entering Sarē Marē but instead made a long detour of the area to get to the city!

Sarē Dubē also excelled Sarē Marē in its chaotic ramblingness. The whole opulent town had the look of a sprawling mushroom growth. Next to the ornate, beautiful and spacious buildings squatted decrepit and shabby mud huts and squalid little box-like objects filled with lower and middle class people. The Harijans, the sweepers and leather workers, lived in unhygienic mud huts with their goat or a skeletal cow which always stood mute and tied to the wooden pegs driven into the ground. These shacks, instead of being out of town as the usual custom was, were in the town amid tall, red-brick buildings owned by the well-to-do people. While these people ate little and went hungry the rich ate milk puddings and delicacies next door, and if the poor happened to be there, their needs were ignored and they were left to look on hungrily with want in their eyes. They had got used to begging and, to try their luck, asked for anything from people's shirts down to their slippers. They would beseech a few drops of milk for their sick children, sometimes paisas by cunningly telling an imaginary tale of woe. But generally people were hardened and would not yield to their entreaties. Asha knew when they lied but she always rewarded them for their ingenuity, generally with money taken from her father's purse. This caused her another type of pain, a pain of guilt and lies, stealing from her own father. The whole town was unsanitary but people had got used to it and did not notice the unhygienic conditions they lived in. Instead of visiting the fields like the Sarē Marē folk did, they used their homes for dry lavatories and the stink was unbearable. These impoverished lavatories were generally a couple of bricks placed in a corner where all the members of the family relieved themselves. If one were unfortunately driven to such a place, the flies flew to one's buttocks, nostrils, mouth and every orifice.

The worst of all fates that could befall women or young girls was to be born sweepers – the young girls and women who cleaned the lavatories for four rupees a month. The men from sweeper castes were extremely indolent and sat about all day in the sun smoking and playing cards. But their poor women would go from door to door collecting heaps of freshly piled, uncovered excrement. This they carried in baskets on their heads, sometimes covered with ashes if the housewife was thoughtful, and sometimes not even with the luxury of that. These young women often had beautiful faces, long dark hair and liquid eyes and yet people forgot that they were also human. They lived in a social system which gave little control and power to them. The rigidity of the caste system was such that it was beyond contemplation for many of them to think that they could escape their allotted positions. The sweepers and the leather workers had no standards to keep up to, they seemed to be content to get what they could without any qualms. But these poor wretches craved for respectability and family honour; they perpetually borrowed and spent on weddings and ceremonies, and gradually sank into debt to outdo their neighbours in the name of tradition. They would spend half their lives accumulating their families and half their lives getting rid of them. They could not drink or gamble, saving and scraping every paisa they could to try to educate their sons.

Their daughters waited patiently, wearily accumulating wrinkles and years of idleness and imprisonment behind four walls, sadly waiting for their parents to release them into the world, waiting for them to find a man, waiting for all their passions, emotions and span of human feelings rigidly stored over the years to be released in the act of matrimony. Meanwhile, they tried to amuse themselves with insipid, crude jokes and wistful longings if ever they saw the shadow of a man, while their mothers pretended daily that their daughters were eternally sixteen. Sometimes an occasional daring one did break loose but it never did her any good. She was ruined for life. The man she ran away with was either a worthless rake, or grew weary of her, trying to get rid of her by selling her to another man, perhaps an old man, who needed a woman, or just sending her to a whorehouse. Once gone she was dead to the family and was never mentioned again by them. After the death of the unlucky fathers who died at an early age in debt, their sons came to carry the same burdens of life, and got trapped in the wheels of the same wretched existence. The wealthy few were very rich. Some of them were moneylenders and others landowners. They were miserly, with even less pity for the poor than the lower-middle-class families. They exploited everyone shamefully, and with their wealth bought the law and any other commodity they wished.

A typical example could be found in the fat, ugly man called Baba Singh. He had married three times and each time his wife had suddenly died of cholera. He owned all the flour, saw and cotton mills in the area, and was a repulsive, balding man with the habit of chewing and biting his nails. People talked in whispers about his morals. They maintained that he went to Bazaar women and also entertained young girls in his house. But when his own daughter refused to enter an arranged marriage in an influential family of his choice and, instead, wished to run away with a young man she was involved with, he shot her through the heart in cold blood. The police came and, after much entertainment, left declaring the murder a suicide. They were well fed with food, drink and money so had to go along with Baba Singh. Of course, later on, some neighbours who had witnessed the shooting talked about it. They said that it was a big hunting gun that he used, and the girl could never have lifted it up, let alone shoot herself through the heart. Baba Singh did not take any notice of these stories and went about making money without a touch of remorse or guilt. His was not an isolated case. Such gruesome incidents were typical in high society, and the police officers, being thoroughly corrupt and underpaid, could be easily bought. They were rarely expected to be the custodians of justice which lay beyond ordinary human beings' reach, in the hands of God. People could helplessly pray twice daily to God to right all their wrongs or go to the temple in search of peace and forgiveness for their never-ending, limitless sins which manifested themselves in an endless cycle of pain and sadness.

Asha's father rented part of a fast dilapidating, rambling mansion of a sometime rich widow who spent most of her time drinking Bhang (ground cannabis leaves) in the company of holy men. She was a skinny, little, shiny-eyed woman with a deep, booming voice, singing praises of the herb, 'God's most cherished, sacred plant' as she called it. One of her friends was called Boota Singh – another holy man. He was employed at Asha's father's school as caretaker cum gardener. But the only plants he lovingly tended were shoulder high cannabis and the only caretaking he did was to look after his pair of goats, running after them and calling them all the time, 'chhey, chhey'. He also drank heavily and would sometimes appear before the headmaster paralytically drunk. As the school had no fenced-off boundaries he also allowed his cronies to graze their cows on the school sports fields, and sometimes these cows wandered in the classrooms and attended lessons. There was a grove of mangoes attached to the school but Boota Singh, being overanxious, would never let them ripen. He had so many pals to distribute unripe mangoes to, and any other produce the ground naturally yielded, that by the time he had made the various forays and rounds the place was utterly barren. But it was a difficult task to get rid of him when all the neighbouring farmers uttered threats that they would set the school on fire, and cut off the headmaster's head.

Boota Singh had thrived in the past, in a state of utter lawlessness, so much so that the past head had become addicted to his hashish. Boota Singh was fond of him and mourned his departure with a great deal of apprehensive anxiety which was, perhaps, well founded. Boota Singh's rule was short-lived, and as soon as the new head was in his post, he was dismissed. He begged to be reinstated; he prayed on his knees that he would never touch a drop of alcohol; he made threats in the last resort, but with all his cannabis plants and piety he departed. After he had left the post, he lingered on in the town and stayed with Akni, the rich widow. His cronies did try to frighten Asha's father by breaking in and burning down his office but to no avail. They could not reinstate him.

Akni's house was dismal and dark, and much infested with rats and gnats. The farm labourers next door lived in equally unhygienic conditions. The women's hair was always infested with lice, and the worst problem was that the chapatti flour bags were infested with fleas and wheat worms. These could not be got rid of, as Asha's father, being quite frugal, made her use up the flour. Sometimes in the dough Asha found them crushed, and this put her off eating. The only source of water was the open well which was set in a narrow, enclosed courtyard. Pigeons roosted above and every other day one of them would fall from its perch into the depths of the well, to drown in the deep, steep darkness. The rats, too, occasionally dived in, so with all this cocktail of savouries the well stand and the water were contaminated and foul. To avert a major disaster, since cholera had killed the neighbour's wife, Raju moved out of Sarē Dubē with Asha and went to live in his school building. Asha was expected to keep house for him and also to pursue her studies. He in turn promised Asha's mother that he would keep a watchful eye over his wayward child.

The school was in the fields away from the village. On one side it was joined by the Muslim burial grounds and since a majority of them had gone to Pakistan these were now flattened and joined on to the school playing fields. The school was controlled and run by a progressive, voluntary body called the *Arya Samaj*. It was controlled, financed and administered by them. The *Arya Samaj* was a reform movement against orthodox Hindu traditions of temple-going and idol worship. The school was established some forty years ago but it had made very little progress and was on the brink of closing down as the voluntary body was losing money. Since the area's population was mostly Sikhs, they preferred to send their children to a Sikh school, two miles away, but the school lingered on with a handful of Hindu boys. Nor had it reached Matriculation standard, only providing education up to middle level, so for the last two years of their studies the boys had to travel some distance or be content with their middle certificate. The environment was neglected and the grounds were over-run by thickly sprawling, prickly desert vegetation and cane. The school office was hardly big enough to squeeze in the headmaster's desk. The furniture was all broken, some of it had pieces missing, and the benches, after constant repairs, were so heavy that they could no longer be lifted. There were four classrooms, their doors and windows painted in faded ink blue – woodworm had attacked them from all sides. They now had great gaps and holes in them and some of them were rapidly falling to pieces. To add to all this, rain seeped through the roof and made everything soaking wet; every year the roof collapsed thanks to the woodworm. There was little equipment in the science labs, not even a balance, while the books in the library were fungified. Their bindings had turned tree-green with mould; wormy and musty pages scattered about all round and even toadstools grew on some of them.

The school did not even own a bell. The old teachers said that they did not need one, since they ended the sessions when they and the boys were tired, and it was usually about 2 pm, while most schools finished at 3. There was a well which did not operate, so there was no immediate sign of the desert being turned into an oasis. The Peon (caretaker) had reared a male buffalo, at much cost to the school, but it was totally work-shy and unless the Peon followed it as it worked the well it sat down. It had excellent hearing and could hear the Peon's footsteps from afar as he cursed and swore at it. He even beat it in frustration sometimes. There were no lavatories but the pupils used the fields nearby. It was also an accepted practice for the local farmers to drive their cattle at noon to the office verandah and let them rest there away from the sun. Sometimes they fed them there with bundles of straw. The herds of goats were allowed to graze in the playing fields and in the mango orchard. When a meeting was in progress the cattle came and joined it with their vacant faces poking in through doors and windows. This was very disconcerting indeed, and when the headmaster ventured to say 'Gulab Singh! Sir, this is a school for your sons not for your cows and goat as well', the man would turn around with angry, glaring eyes, and retort, 'I have been doing this for fifty years. Who are you, anyway, to stop me? You wait till someone cracks your pumpkin head, telling us off like that. We are not your school kids.' The threats were particularly nasty sometimes; 'I shall set this school on fire and roast you in it too. You pig of a Brahmin!'

But gradually these onslaughts grew less, and there was no longer dung all over the paths or goat-droppings or straw. The situation was improving; the well was now working though the harness for the buffalo was stolen every now and then. New roofs were being put on, and most of the digging was done by gangs of students in the evenings and mornings. Later on they were given jugs of milk to drink in order to refresh them for further labour. There was a lot of activity about in those days – and a sense of excitement to live in the noisy clamour and hive of activity. It seemed that something great was going to happen. The paths were being made, weeds dug up and flower beds planted. The meagre store of books was catalogued, dusted, polished and new ones were ordered. To Asha it appeared as if there was a gigantic wave of co-operation sweeping through the young people and adults. This new spirit led a lot of new boys to enrol and soon they had divided themselves into workgangs, digging the earth with a fierce force, carving out of a tumbledown building and sand dunes, magnificent football pitches, volley ball courts and playgrounds. The youths had found a constructive focus for their energies and were happy to channel them into tangible results. It was good for Asha to see her father as the Creator, the Hero of it all. It made her feel so proud of him as she identified with his achievements. She worshipped him and hoped that she was worthy enough to be his daughter. Soon the school was to be promoted to a high school level on condition that it had an enrolment of 800 students who paid fees. The present numbers were still abysmally low. The majority of the pupils were from the lower castes and too poor to pay. Many years later, Asha still remembered that grand summer when her father spent every spare minute walking on foot for miles to neighbouring villages persuading the poor farmers and the rich landowners to send their children to their own local school.

Asha went on some journeys with him and knew how tiresome and exhausting they were. Her father's feet used to be blistered as he walked in temperatures of a hundred and more, and at night he was too exhausted to go to sleep. In the dusky twilight of the evening he would return tired and weary but satisfied, when the only thing he needed was a basin full of ice-cold water for his feet. Then he would eat his meal hurriedly and start coaching pupils free of charge in the long, lamplit nights. He worked with missionary zeal. It seemed that he had no existence apart from his school. He rarely visited the rest of his family at Sarē Marē, and when he did it was a brief, hurried visit. In the mornings he got up at 5 am and helped Asha to learn the rules of English grammar or taught her Indian history. Then at six when the dawn was breaking, father and daughter went to the fields, and on the way they gathered a bundle of dry sticks for cooking. There were no kitchen facilities in the school but they had improvised some in the school shed. The shed was often filled with smoke and Raju's eyes would run and get red as he blew and persevered with the dwindling fire. The only other firewood they burnt were broken, worm-eaten benches and desks; these produced large quantities of smoke but not much heat. Asha, at thirteen, had little idea of cooking; she had never been told to do a thing in the kitchen by her mother. The first meal she prepared for her father and herself was a memorable one: the chapattis were dog-eared and the lentils were full of stones. She felt ashamed but her father ate them gratefully without a word of complaint. On subsequent days, her cooking improved but it was mainly due to her father's careful instruction, supervision and encouragement.

The greatest problem for Asha was the lack of privacy or a toilet. Sometimes she thought her bladder would burst. During the school hours the school was over-run with boys and it was impossible for Asha to find a corner to urinate in peace without being seen or spied upon. She was a shy girl: sometimes she had to go a full day without urinating, until the pain in her stomach and bladder was too unbearable. Later on the new Peon improvised a thatched cover, much like a wigwam, so it was less difficult for Asha although she was still aware that a hundred pairs of eyes knew where she was heading. She also learnt to ride her father's cycle, much to the amazement of boys and the general public. She was notable as the only girl in a boys' school.

Raju was always occupied with school affairs, so most of the time Asha was left alone. From 8.30 till 3 pm she sat on the cold tin box in her father's office. She sat there with a few books, trying to study, and all the time she looked out through the windows and watched the boys going to and fro. Big, ugly boys in colourful clothes and turbans; thin, starved boys in rags; handsome boys with wicked, smiling eyes. The office was busy all day long with people who swarmed to talk to her father, and she sat there silent and observant, day after day in that lonely corner, perched like a chicken. In the morning she watched the very black sweeper come, pretending to sweep the leaves with a long swing of his broom. He was called Kutta (young buffalo) and he looked like one. He would shout greetings to Asha and it always went along like this:

'Good Morning, Little Miss.'

'Good Morning, Kutta, how is the wife?'

'Fine.'

'How are the children?'

'Fine.'

'And, how are you?'

'Fine.'

She watched the new Peon harness the lazy buffalo which stopped moving as soon as it heard his footsteps go away. The Peon was a retired soldier from the army. He was a good gardener and grew the most wonderful spread of marigolds, daisies, pyrethrums, cornflowers and giant lupins and sunflowers. He also planted bananas outside the office verandah. It was largely due to his efforts that the whole place sometimes looked like a paradise with flowers, birds and butterflies. Sweet-scented jasmine and champak grew all around, and at night in the moonlight the white flowers glowed enchantingly and the wafting sweet scent lulled Asha in a faraway land of dreams. In the early morning the tight buds would unfold and display the fragile white petals as if they had just wakened and were yawning. The Peon was called 'Fauji' (army man) though his real name must have been something else. He had a crescent tattooed on his forehead. He smoked Red Lamp cigarettes and dressed in an old uniform. He always addressed Asha's father in the army fashion, calling him 'Sir', 'Sahib', clicking his heels and standing to attention. But he had one great drawback – he could never spend the night at school. He was terrified in case his former enemies carried out their threats to kill him. So there had to be a night watchman too. And it proved expensive. The Peon was from a lower caste – a cobbler's son – so naturally some people resented his office. But he was the most efficient man Asha knew. He could do anything and do it well. He always dressed in old khaki and wore big army boots. He was the person who taught her to ride her father's bike and ran after her for miles holding the carrier while she pedalled. But he had a weakness for liquor and one day, much to Asha's sadness, after having been found drunk he was dismissed. Asha could not make her father changed his mind – he detested indiscipline and drinking – the orchards and flower beds were never so dazzling after that.

Sometimes on Sundays Asha and her father went to visit their home at Sarē Marē. The road was unmade, barely a footpath. It ran through the fields in a zig-zag, uneven and sandy, rough and pitted. The area was semi-desert with no trees, shrubs or bushes for shade or any water. But Asha's father would make her sit on the handle bar of his bike and balance a huge dirty bundle of washing at the back, and then try to get on the saddle and pedal. It took a lot of effort for him to heave and push through the wilderness – he often had punctures – so by the time he neared the village he was utterly exhausted. It was not easy for Asha's circulation or her bottom which always got bruised and sore so that she could hardly bear to sit down. The procession that the father and daughter made on the bike was of much interest and speculation to the other passersby and villagers. It had become a well-known show for most of them to look for the Master on the bike with his mature daughter. So, mostly when they neared a village, Asha would get down and walk so as not to create too much of a spectacle.

They passed Burko where she saw crowds of people washing clothes in a pond, and then bathing themselves and even drinking water. After another fifteen minutes they would pass through another village called Badallon. On both sides of the village there were Harijan houses, surrounded by manure heaps, open drains, excrement and other foul stenches they had to endure. The children wandered about undressed, had conjunctivitis and boils and starved pot bellies as they played and rolled in the dirt. Their poor cattle showed their rib cages as they stayed put in one place, tethered, surrounded by a mixture of dung, mud and urine. Their menfolk sat on charpoys, looking calm and contented, gently puffing at their hukkahs, and lazily watching any activity on the road. Asha had to hold her nose to pass through this area. It made her wonder why these were the people who generally cleaned up other people's houses and filth but wouldn't bother with their own. In stark contrast there was the odd mud hut where a genuine effort had been made to beautify the surroundings. The walls were immaculately plastered with ochre and dung, with marigolds growing all around. Such a house would help Asha to forget the shabbiness that surrounded her, and made her feel that life was not all toil. At the end of the village there was such a little house near a clean little pond, and in front of it grew pumpkins and flowers, while a little spotted deer ran around shaking its tail in the front yard.

When she reached her home, all the spaciousness she had imagined would recede; each time the house would shrink and look narrower and smaller. Perhaps it was the impact of green stretches of vast fields that made the house shrink or perhaps it was that she had forgotten how small it really was. As usual her mother, dusty-eyed, dusty-haired and dusty-handed, would come running to the door to welcome them through the cowshed where she would be diligently separating chaff from dust, mixing it with cow cake, flour and clover for the cows. The process was a difficult one which needed patience and time. It affected her eyes and made them perpetually red and watery and she frequently had a bad cough in the winter. But the farmers, when they crushed the straw, mixed heaps of soil with it and sold it by weight in order to make a profit, and did not pay much attention to the health of the cattle or people who had to sieve it all again. Asha's mother often complained that purity had disappeared since most people's standards of honesty had left them, and the farmers were no exception. If they sold clarified butter they put one-third of whey and vegetable compound in it; if they sold wheat it would have one-third of barley and gram in it. This dishonesty was a part of all big and small businesses and the family could trust no one, branding them all as cheats. Even the milk was watered down. Asha had seen it for herself when her neighbour mixed the goat's milk with water.

Most of Raju's staff had inherited a tradition of fixing examinations from the old days. But in the old headmaster's time there were no university examinations or boards and success was only a matter of give and take – so he would give a boy a pass for a

118

fixed sum of money. In fact the examination times were named 'harvest festival' by the old man. 'The farmer works hard and in the end fills his house with grain, cotton and sugar; he works hard and therefore has the right to fill, if not overflow, his house with whatever he can get.' That was the argument he used on Raju. The rest of the teachers, too, were free to follow this example. So, in other grades too, there were 100 per cent passes. The teachers did well and then gambled some of this money at a local gambling den. Raju was taken aback when he first came to know of this system and, like a reformer, set about abolishing this practice with a fanatical zeal, but all he succeeded in doing was making all his staff his sworn enemies. They could not believe that a headmaster could be honest and survive on the low salary he got. They felt that perhaps the size of the gratuities were not big enough for him and persuaded some of the parents to beseech his aid and a 'pass' for their son with the help of a hundred rupee note. But even this was not acceptable to the new headmaster.

The revolt against him gradually began to spread. The leader was the deputy head who was near to retiring age, passed over for headship, and never recognised for his contribution to the school. He set out to seek revenge, for hadn't Raju humiliated him enough in front of the new teachers and the pupils? Bedi Das had been in the school for thirty years and was a faithful servant, and when Raju got the job he thought at least he would be guided by Bedi's experience. Raju strictly forbade him to accept any gifts or bribes, and when sometimes Bedi fell asleep in the class Raju was rude to him and mocked him – his name for him was the Opium Taker! The Opium Taker felt more and more poisonous and this is how he set out to destroy Raju:

The story spans many years but briefly it went as follows. The deputy head had many consultations with his old colleagues who all had a grudge against Raju and his holier-than-thou attitudes. They set out to compile a list of possible doubtful cases where the headmaster may himself have taken bribes or misused his position of authority. They wished to gather as much evidence as they could, and if they were unsuccessful they used bribery to persuade people to come up with fictitious stories. Later these false charges were embroidered upon, and fraudulent papers were even produced. In one or two cases the headmaster's signature was copied. Bedi Das had a major hand in this witchhunt; it had taken him months to compile the charge sheet. On the surface Bedi Das was one of those proverbial meekly spoken, humble men, who are always joining their hands together in blessing, prayer and submissiveness but inwardly he was like Duryodhna – the classical villain. In the school Raju's position was again isolated; he felt lonely, bewildered and alienated. He believed in his work alone and had no time for hearsay and rumours. He had little inkling that a deadly plot was being hatched against him, and he had few friends among the staff.

One day, out of the blue, he was summoned to the city where the management committee had its head office. There he was shown a lengthy list of charges against him; it was a sudden shock which left him utterly bewildered and nonplussed. This was the first time he fully understood that developing an honest policy and work principles in a society which was over-run with corruption was tantamount to creating his own deadly enemies. But the old chairman had faith in Raju – he knew him so well – and trusted his integrity, but he also warned him that he was ready to retire soon and the person likely to replace him could be bought easily. Raju had been a popular and well-loved teacher among his pupils but he was a poor judge of character and overstrict in his dealings with people. He was often unapproachable and incommunicative so the rest of the teachers hated him for his arrogance and his gruff, insulting, sarcastic manner. Bedi Das and others stored up all the insults and lobbied others who said, 'We'll show him yet. If he is not out of this chair soon we are not men but mice!' They also went to a number of self-styled community leaders and asked for their support. Raju was not liked by these men: he never ingratiated himself with them, never sat with them on Sundays or conversed with them. He did not puff at their communal hukkah – or enjoy malicious gossip and rumour. He did not accept gifts or promote unworthy teachers and students. The zeal of Bedi Das and others resulted in a petition signed by a few of these mighty men, and this was anonymously dispatched to the school governors. So this battle continued causing anger and irritation to Raju; he never knew what would come next from these jugglers' bags. It was ironic that these teachers were determined to prove that the headmaster was corrupt while they were doing all the corrupting, and throughout all this wrangle Raju sat night after night burning his own kerosene oil to coach his weak pupils as usual so that he could obtain 100 per cent passes for his school.

The Matriculation pupils had to go to an examination centre two miles away at Dalleba to take their examinations. There was always a lot of activity for the examinations. The weak students would continue to revise pages full of English up to the last minute. Some worked on hunches and memorised whole essays on popular topics such as 'A Rainy Day', 'A Football Match', 'What I like reading best'. These were the themes which had appeared for a number of years in English examinations and sometimes the guesses would pay off and sometimes not, but come what may, the students would write down the essay they had memorised and consequently fail.

There were times when the supervisors had been physically attacked and even assassinated. These were the times when a dozen or so students would be thrown out of the centres for copying and cheating. The methods of copying were also novel and varied. One boy related how he had written all the propositions in geometry in the folds of his shalwar, and had managed to copy the right ones. Some of them hid books in their laps, papers in their socks, or copied from the fellow sitting next to them by arrangement. Indeed, many times, when discovered cheating, several of them swallowed whole sheets of paper. Sometimes the books were hidden in lavatories and though an invigilator escorted the party, he too was often found to be collaborating. Once when Raju was the head of the largest centre he found one of the invigilators filling in a map for one of his geography pupils. Raju wholeheartedly deprecated these means but the students and the teachers were so used to cheating and had so many different ways of fixing the answers that, to his disappointment, not a great deal could be achieved – and the system remained. He felt it was his duty as a leader to work hard to change the system as there was no other option. So each year hundreds of students were found out and disqualified, and thousands were never discovered. Raju was also the external examiner for some centres, and although all these papers were strictly confidential, had coded numbers and came direct from the university by registered mail, people could still trace him through red tape and corruption, and many hopeful parents who thought they could buy a qualification for their child knocked at his door. It was sad and shameful to see the position of these people: many had daughters of marriageable age and sorely needed a piece of paper. They arrived at Raju's doorstep with a dirty wad of notes discreetly hidden in their palms but all of them went back – some disappointed, others indignant – thinking that he was perhaps greedier and wanted more.

Raju's problem was that he was patently honest and could neither give nor take a bribe. He often recounted the episode when he was persuaded to offer a bribe when he was a young, inexperienced assistant master. It was a memorable occasion, a rare government inspection made by an official government inspector from the State Education Board. He felt that he needed a praiseworthy report on his teaching so that he could ask for a much-needed pay rise. So his wife persuaded him to take a few baskets of fruit before he went to fetch the school log book with the inspector's comments. As ill luck would have it, the inspector was not at home so Raju entrusted the baskets to a servant and came home worried, wondering if he had done the right thing. Raju was a light sleeper and a great worrier, and if he had something on his mind he would usually pass the night awake. So after many sleepless nights he decided to visit the inspector and call for his 'log book'. He was really embarrassed to meet the man face to face; he dared not look up and meet his eyes but all the time kept thinking about the two baskets of fruit and whether the inspector would refer to them. He very much hoped that he would not. Towards the end of the interview the inspector cleared his throat and Raju sensed straightaway that he was going to say something about the wretched fruit. The inspector light-heartedly began, 'By the way, your bananas are lying on the table in the verandah. It was kind of you to bring them. The children ate the oranges up although they were a bit on the sour side. But here is some money to compensate you. It is not my habit to accept gifts.' Raju never forgot this highly embarrassing scene and was firmer than ever in his decision never to give or take a bribe. He stuck to this throughout his life.

Preparations for the grand opening of a new wing and verandahs were going on. The school secretary and the president and other honoured guests were invited. A huge canopy hung like a vast red and yellow dome, it waved and fluttered on the resplendent bamboo poles. Colourful bunting and banners hung everywhere. A raised dais was set up for the honoured guests, and rows of comfortable chairs were specially bought for the day. There sat the distinguished guests – fat-bellied, pouch-faced, hook-nosed, foul-breathed with too much garlic and raw onions in their diet, gold-rimmed spectacled; the corrupt officials sat smoothing their beards and turbans, twisting their moustaches and looking around to note and be noticed, gently coughing and clearing their throats. The ground was sprinkled with rose water and strewn with soft, silken flower petals. Early in the morning a holy fire was lit with incense burning in a brass pot on the dais, and mantras were chanted for the well-being of the school and its continued future prosperity. Later on, speeches were made and progress reports read, and enthusiastic crowds of boys all dressed in saffron uniforms, for it was Baisakhi (spring festival), recited poems and sang songs, and they were all in praise of Raju and his school. Instead of pleasing the dignitaries, the managers and other status seekers, the thrust of the eulogies was directed at the headmaster. They felt insulted and ignored. Why were their names not included in the homages? So they sat there stiff in black Achkans, never cheering, never smiling and never uttering a word. Later on, however, they became less stiff when they were invited to have a guided tour of the new building, and there they were shown the Honours List – names of all the dignitaries who had contributed. Now they were very heavily garlanded and thanked by the head-master, and later on were given a sumptuous dinner. Despite all this indulgence most seemed somewhat awed and distanced perhaps by the overall honesty and impeccable truthfulness of Raju as he stood there dressed in homespun clothes looking simple and dignified. They had not wished him to achieve such glorious success in this project, and he had never approached them with any difficulties or problems and now they seemed to have no role. One of the chief dignitaries, the President, who had been a refugee from Pakistan, wanted Raju to hire one of his sons as a teacher but the son had a poor work record and was totally unsuitable and Raju would not agree. The President then systematically set out to make Raju pay for his stand, and filled his life with petty harassments and anxieties. He would ask him to come to the city to meet him at short notice and at odd times. He brought in so many sets of new rules and restrictions that life was made really unpleasant for Raju and his autonomy was taken away. He could not do anything without referring to the corrupt little man.

In the end Raju made a momentous decision: he decided to give up the school he had built from scratch. He wrote his resignation and threw away his headship and all that he had worked for. The greatest wrench he felt was to sever the connection with the boys he taught and loved so much, and who adored him for his honesty and integrity and his undying devotion to hard work. He decided that he would never teach again, and tore up his teaching qualifications gained after so much hard work and toil. He never looked for another post. But through this painful experience, he was irrevocably altered. It seemed that something had prematurely gone out of his life, leaving him tired and lonely, and he would sit for hours, passive, utterly quiet and desolate, and listen to his watch tick. It seemed as if he had fulfilled his life's mission and there was nothing else for him to do. He still got up very early and sang songs about Rama, performed a hundred tasks he always did, but it was never the same again. A part of his life had gone and he was listless and strange. It seemed as if his life from now on was to be empty and he lived simply because the wish to live remained. A precious and creative part of him had been destroyed. It hurt him to talk about the school or his role in its development, and if someone started talking about it he would suddenly go very quiet and say, 'Please don't, let us not talk about these events. Nothing good comes out of it. Let us say that I did my bit, and they theirs.' He lost interest in most things including his children. He no longer tutored them in languages, history, geography and religion. He just let them do as they wished, and went on looking and living.

I sat upon an ice-cold stone in the rosy dawn waiting for you to appear like a hero from the mist, cold and dewy, to appear like the sun or the morning star, or the curling twist of the morning smoky fire, or the shrill crowing of a distant cock, or a half-opened jasmine bud newly washed, sweet-scented and pure. With a prayer in my heart I waited. Did he come? No, he did not. Far, far away he fled from a fanciful mind and slept soundly in the land of dreams. He was not a mortal, he was no living being, he was part of a dream. Then I replaced my love with a mortal being and the Book said that was the Law. Why did I not question it? Laws are not to be questioned. I found the experience bittersweet, and I waited for it to turn sweeter for I still wanted to capture it, in a touch, a smile, big bright eyes and a dark brown fat nose on pimple-strewn face. Then the sweetness of my love turned sour, although still tinged with sweetness. Yet the feelings emerged strongly, powerfully, like a bird swooping down at dusk, and tormented me through the still, rainy nights until I could stay quiet no longer, and I cried in pain and fear, 'God!, what is this you are giving to me?' And God answered 'Out of darkness emanates light, and out of light comes love but you must pass through the tunnel of darkness first to get to the light.' But I did not recognise God's voice then so I laughed.

I a little haven of your delights
Wish that you could be my wife!

'I shall not be your wife nor anyone's wife for I cannot give my soul away, and I shall never marry a man whom I do not fully love.' But you promised to come back. 'Wait, let me go to a foreign land and come back to you with my fortune made!'

I kept my promise. For three long years I was a slave to my dream, and waited for you. Recalled day and night your child face and big bushbaby eyes. I loved your spotty cheeks so I told my mother I would only marry you. My mother agreed that I could. She knew that I would forget and that you too were of the same chain as me. Then one day, without a word, you dropped in. You were speculating, hoping to settle down with a good wife, but you were that image no more. Your big bushbaby eyes were without light; they shone no longer; they had faded into nothingness and ordinariness. You looked shrunken and yet prosperous; you wore a tailored suit, and tie and smart shoes. You had achieved the respectability that money can buy. But I did not know you. I allowed you to kiss me in the memory of my childhood long past but I did not stir; you seemed ordinary and of the earth. All the dreaming and waiting was worth more than what you had become. So I let you go bearing the marks of rejection, howling, raving mad, a mere mortal man made of flesh with bony knuckles and sticking out ears, hairy-fingered, with lots of hair, a mad man whose socks smelt.

Yet I never forgot the man of my dreams. You were my first love – a longing without fulfilment, a curious mixture of fantasy and myth. Yet I refused to experience you. You came like the rain at a dry, desert period of my life, I a young sapling bent towards you – you were like the dew to a thirsty young bud. But neither you nor I knew what loving really was. So I went my way and you went yours. I remember you now with tenderness and emotion for who knows, had you chained me, I might have eaten you up. Our two paths shall never meet again, and I will never know what became of you, and we shall both grope in the darkness for the Light.

Balik Singh's great wealth was well known in the village, as was his reputation for meanness. He had a father who was over a hundred years old. He caused Balik Singh great disappointment and expend-iture by demanding a new pair of shoes each year. Although Balik Singh prayed for his demise, the old man, for more than half a century, had worked hard and amassed a fortune for Balik Singh by lending money on a 50 per cent rate of interest. He was an excellent usurer who saved every paisa he made and, during the big slump after the war, bought a large portion of arable land in the village. At that time the land was cheap and belonged to the farmers who went bankrupt and later some of them hanged themselves for shame. But the means did not matter to the old man, and later when his son came to inherit the family fortune he easily beat his father in meanness and ruthlessness. After Raju had the episode with the highway robbers he came to assist him and encourage him at the time of his misfortune. Raju and his family were only too glad to have someone advise them about the new situation and the legal system they knew little about. Later Balik Singh became a regular visitor to the house. He looked pious with this snow-white beard and little, greenish, shrew eyes, and his white, tight turban. He always looked humble and caring; there was a meekness in his demeanour, in the way he walked and talked. He said that he called because he felt the need for the enlightened company of Master Ji's daughters, who read poetry so beautifully and also wrote letters for him. He usually came carrying a rose or two as gifts and lounged about on the palang (sofa bed) until such time he felt he ought to go. He also managed to obtain two bags of cement for Master Sahib, and later on kept reinforcing his position by reminding Raju of his great kindness by saying: 'You remember that time when your roof fell down, good job I managed to get you some cement. I really wonder what you would have done about it in the rainy season, eh?' At this Raju would again acknowledge his gratitude rather reluctantly and painfully. But in the end Raju became so burdened listening to the same old tale that he decided that he would do anything in his power to repay him so that he would not speak of it again. Anyhow, one summer day, Balik Singh visited Sarē Dubē and went to the Master's home. Raju was away but Asha was studying at home. Balik Singh said that he was so pleased to see the 'youthful' girl and had brought some oranges for her. Asha excused herself to make some tea for him, as was customary, but he shouted from the room, 'Don't bother, come and sit down with me, my child.' Asha did as she was told but there was something about Balik Singh that made her nervous. It was the way he looked at her. Soon the old man was pulling the trembling and nervous Asha towards him and trying to kiss and bite her lips. The girl found this behaviour difficult to understand: Balik Singh was an old friend of the family but he should not be behaving in such a way. Now he was burrowing and pushing his tongue in her mouth, and she hated the old man for his pushing and fumbling. He had introduced an element into her life of which she was only vaguely conscious. His actions were so sudden and forceful she did not know how to handle him, so she stayed reluctantly quiet and submissive as though nothing had taken place. After Balik Singh had left she was full of torment and guilt; she also felt angry and violated too. She scrubbed her face and mouth with copious quantities of soap but the red-faced man and his touch still lingered on. Asha had heard stories and rumours about the old man, that he had an eye for young women, but she had never seen him in this role. Besides he always called Asha 'daughter'. After much hesitation Asha decided not to let the old man get his own lustful way with her. So next time he tried kissing her Asha bit his tongue quite badly. He was angry but also full of excuses. His explanation was that he loved Asha in the western tradition and did not mean any harm. But Asha asked him to keep his western traditions to himself. After that encounter Balik Singh stopped visiting Master Ji's house. The rest of the family wondered what they had done to offend him but Asha left them to guess and never told them the tale of the 'kissing Grandfather in the western tradition'. But Raju was grateful that he did not have to hear any more stories of the favours done to him in the nick of time.

Episodes such as these were a common experience for many girls. Since they had no access to young men of their own age, older men, often trusted and loved by the family, misused the trust placed in them. Many girls accepted these attentions, but many who kept quiet did so because they felt that their families would somehow hold them responsible for what took place. Asha had to cope with many such unsolicited advances. The worst one was the time when she escorted her father to a neighbouring village to conduct some external examinations. They stayed in a respectable family home with a man who practised homeopathy. He was known as Vaid Ji but as uncle to Asha. Much to her great alarm, one day she found him kneeling over her while she was asleep. His weight had effectively pinned her to the bed and he was desperately trying to remove her clothing. She told him that she would yell and wake everyone up if he did not leave. At first he did not believe her and kept pushing his erect genitals at her until she kicked him hard. The kick landed well and he left. But the fortnight turned into a nightmare as she did not wish for her father to be distressed during examinations. Vaid Ji had children of Asha's age and a very pretty wife and yet he pursued Asha with great vehemence. He would pounce on her during the day time, evening or afternoon whenever she was alone. In the end the trauma became too much for her – she developed a high temperature and sickness. She wondered how she had managed to save her virginity through all this, but worse still she learnt not to trust any older men.

GRANDMA PALIKA AND THE SPIRIT OF THE ANCESTORS

Grandma Palika's house stood in a very crowded part of the village. It was an ancient, decaying, unstable, shaky house of brick. The bricks were all individually made by hand, so one could see their uneven dimensions. The interior of the house had old, yellowing walls, covered with ancient cracks. They criss-crossed the house like lines on a map. The heavy, carved front door of the house had turned a shiny black with the years, while the brass studs in it had turned jade green. It creaked on its hinges and was reluctant to move. Grandma Palika bathed the hinges with mustard oil, so over the years the sill and the steps had acquired a patina of shiny glaze. On the sides of the giant, ancient door were two alcoves in which stood two giant, dignified bulls. They too were carved out of wood and were ebony black. One of them had an eye missing and on holy days Grandma Palika used to light a candle in this empty eye socket, and the house looked weird from the outside with one of the bull's eyes on fire. The back of the house had low, dark rooms and each room had a low door with similar bulls (Siva's carriers) resting in the alcoves, but their sizes diminished with each door and in the last room the bulls were only the size of an owl. Grandma Palika would light little lamps of ghee on their backs. The lamps would burn softly with flickering flames, and at that time the decaying house would assume a palatial look like a fairy land. But during the day the rooms were unnaturally dark like deep little dungeons, and to enter the depths of their darkness was a courageous act. Grandma Palika had a number of mahogany, built-in cupboards which stood on little legs in each room, and if Asha went in alone she always imagined something silently, creepingly, stealthily rushing at her, ready to twist her little neck, reaching out of the cavern-like gloom of the deep dungeonous cupboards.

The house had a cool kitchen. The corners were piled high with brass pots and pans and other utensils of various shapes and sizes. In one corner there was a little handmill, the handle of which was worn out where many female hands, including my mother's, had rested, so now it was polished smooth and shiny with age. In the groove one could see and count all the fingers and the fat thumb at the top. In the far corner there was a small cupboard in the wall from which came the sweet scent of incense and faded jasmine and roses. In it were Grandma Palika's Gods, Goddesses and deities of the temple. Here Lord Krishna had a smile on his lips, big black eyes, long eyelashes and curls falling right to his waist. He seemed strangely alive and sometimes it seemed as if his lips moved and started to say something. There was a marble Lingam, the symbol of creation belonging to Lord Siva – the Lord Creator of the Universe. It was in the shape of an ordinary, rounded white stone. There was the fierce Goddess Kali, riding on a tiger. She was cut out of black ebony with her red tongue hanging out of her cadaverous mouth as her flared nostrils almost twitched in anger. There was also the gentle Lakshmi with her four arms, perched demurely on her lotus seat. The seat was now red with vermilion for she had been much worshipped over hundreds of Deewalis. There were Rama, Sita and Lakshman, the trio, on one seat. Apart from these main Gods and Goddesses, Grandma had a hoard of others whom she could not identify, but all the same they were holy. In the bottom shelf she kept her *Gita* and the *Ramayana* tied in red and yellow pieces of silk with tassels on them. Immediately underneath the cupboard was a four-legged stool. It was very old and battered. If one leaned on it, it creaked, squeaked and jerked. Grandma used it for her idols, and near it lay a woollen mat, its edges frayed and full of holes, which she used for sitting crosslegged on while praying.

Immediately behind the kitchen was a little room like a prison cell. It had no windows in it and the dark in this room was somehow more formidable and solid. It hung like a curtain as if one could touch and feel it. It was here that Grandma Palika spent all her long, lonely winter evenings and nights. She had a little, light, bamboo charpoy in it, only big enough for her and besides it was easy to carry and she preferred it to a full-sized bed. She did not wear any night clothes, she said they hurt her. Instead she would go about wrapped in a coarse, white, homespun sheet, and in the distant dark she looked like a ghost. During the summer she took this charpoy upstairs on the roof to sleep near her holy plant which she called Mother Tulsi. It was just an ordinary scented herb which grew in profusion in the woods but Grandma attributed celestial qualities to it. She was full of myths and legends – strange stories about the potency of the plant with its holy qualities. When in the end she killed it by overwatering with blessed water, over which long prayers were said, she did not discard the dead Tulsi. Instead she wrapped every dead petal and seed in choicest silk and patiently waited for the final rites when she could personally take it and submerge and fuse its soul with the holy waters of the Great Mother–Ganges.

Come winter, come summer, Grandma would always spend her day in the front room which was light and airy. She would leave the front door open, and during spinning sessions she would peep out every now and then and observe every passerby. Grandma was the loneliest and most isolated little woman. She lived alone in that haunted house where the spirits of the dead freely fluttered, roamed and haunted her like so many shadows and apparitions. But this exile was of her own choosing. She was exceedingly stubborn and would not have it any other way. She had three independent sons with their families and a hoard of grandchildren, but she deliberately chose to live in the house where she first came as a young bride. After the death of Grandfather she stayed in that house with her middle son who shared the house with her. Later he made his own money and wished to build himself a house fitting his position, but Grandma Palika stayed put. She said that she did not get on with the younger generation, she being keen on discipline and old-fashioned values while they called her 'queer' with her old ideas about decency, dress and hair. They did not give her due respect or listen to her advice, making Grandma Palika very unhappy, so she fought for her independence and stayed on alone in the old house. At times Raju and his wife entreated her to move in with them but Grandma said, 'I don't want to be a rolling stone in my old age, son, besides, I would like to die where your father died and where he first brought me as his bride.' There were always pride, tears and determination in her voice; so she chose her independence and her utter loneliness. The painful subject was never mentioned again. Though Grandma was keen to have one of her grandchildren to stay with her and Asha, who adored Grandma Palika, would have been only too pleased to go to her, her mother would not let her go. Asha would often dream about staying in the rambling old house alone with her Grandmother for she liked the courage of the old lady, loved reading to her and listening to her wonderful old tales. So Grandma lived on all alone in the overcrowded part of the village where she was seen as a sarcastic and bitter old woman.

Grandma Palika had almond-shaped eyes striking in their keenness as she peered at a person through her rounded, brass-rimmed glasses. Her glasses had owlish, glittering frames and gripping sides which she tucked neatly around her ears. Their constant use had made a deep indentation in the top of her nose, and she used to wrap a piece of cottonwool around the thin wire. Her forehead was high like a dome, her face wrinkled and a little like a shrunken red apple. Her skin was very fair, she had a hook nose and thin lips. She had no teeth in her mouth and chewed with her gums, making strange clicking noises like a child. Her voice quivered heavily and sometimes it almost broke midway in a sentence, while her head shook. Her flesh hung loose over her arms and body like frills, and her breasts hung nearly to her knees because of her hunch back. She tied her thin, snow-white hair in a neat bun at the nape of her thin, scrawny, wrinkled neck. Yet Grandma Palika was resilient. She was given to a hard life of industry and toil. By sheer force of will she performed all the tasks she had done when she was young. In her late eighties she went out in the June sun and picked cotton like a young girl. She was quick of movement and neat in her step. Apart from spinning all day, she still used the handmill for her own ground wheat flour, and also for the holy people who swarmed around her and asked for alms. No one ever went empty handed from her home. She was scrupulously clean and tidy and always scrubbed the old brasses until they shone in the dark, and every corner of the old house was spotless. Her few homespun, coarse clothes were always clean. Her day began at four for she could not sleep for more than four or five hours. After an early morning cold bath she would squat on her mat on the bare, scrubbed floor and lovingly bring her army of gods and goddesses out. She would bathe them, polish them and sing praises to them. Grandma could not read but all the same she undid her books and sat before them silent and humble telling her rosary. After the prayers were over the sun came up and she would bring out a brass pitcher of water to pay homage to the Sun God, then she would hurry to a neighbour's pump to carry water for her daily needs. She would light a fire in her hearth, make her breakfast and always share it with a stray dog. After washing the dishes, she would do some spinning or grinding or any other chore that needed her attention till night would come round again to wrap her busy day with a prayer. She also went to religious gatherings to visit holy saints and to pay periodic visits to the ancestral tombs. Though the ancestors were all cremated, a place was reserved for them, in each of their names, on the outskirts of the village. Grandma Palika would put on her full black skirt with the red tassels proudly dangling on the side to march there arrogantly in her coarse shoes with a few choice dishes. Sometimes it was halwa, sometimes just milk and sometimes rice pudding. She occasionally took Asha with her, and they marched through unploughed fields and long grass until they came to a pond which was shaded by giant trees and its surface covered with giant lotus flowers. After tripping dangerously over some planks which served as a rickety bridge the grandmother and the granddaughter would come to a little mound all overgrown with thorn scrub laden with scarlet berries. Grandma would squeeze through the tangle of the thorny undergrowth and sometimes tear her duppatta, and her arms too would generally get scratched. She would take off her shoes then walk gingerly, avoiding the thorns and the thistles, to the low, domed entrance. She would crouch in the doorway and then disappear inside.

It was a low, whitewashed, temple-shaped monument but Asha dreaded it and dared not enter its precincts. Grandma would deftly bring out some dough in the utter darkness and mould a well-shaped lamp and fill it with ghee. Then she would roll a piece of cottonwool into a wick and light it before the entrance; she would arrange some of the dainties there and ask for the ancestral blessings. As soon as she left the cobras and the grass snakes smelt the food and came hissing for milk, then Grandma said that the ancestors were pleased and had accepted her gifts and blessed her house, while overhead the black ravens and Brahmini kites circled greedily for their share.

On the way back at the edge of the pond Grandma stopped and bowed to the Goddess Sheetla. She recounted how many children were lost to the wraith of the Goddess during the last outbreak of smallpox. Asha often wondered why the gods and goddesses were cruel and why they chose to punish children and adults so often, but if she asked this question Grandma would cry out: 'Hush child, it's their way of retribution. How else do the mortals know of their power?'

'Grandma, why don't our ancestors do something about the crows, ravens and snakes? I don't think they are there, if they were wouldn't they do something about them?'

'You're just like the rest of them, child. I have seen the gods and their powers with my own eyes.' And then she would start telling Asha the same old and much repeated stories. Stories about the past exploits and glories of such and such male ancestors. Women were never mentioned, as if they did not exist, as if they did not give birth to them, as if they played no part in their existence and upbringing. The episodes related their past deeds of charity, of selflessness, about how great and good they were. And how, after death, though they became a part of God, their souls being Brahmin did not fail to descend and share her gifts, and now they watched over all our deeds and severely chastised any shortcomings on our part, and how nothing was ever hidden from their ever-wakeful, watchful eyes – an awesome prospect indeed to contemplate. She maintained that she did not go there all that weary way just for herself but for the general well-being of all her children and their families to ask for forgiveness for her irreligious and non-believing modern day children. On reaching the house Grandma would suddenly forget about all these colourful tales and she would seem to wake from the world of the dead and start darting about to make a meal or a cup of tea.

In the narrow, congested and ill-designed street which ran up in a snaky, zig-zag fashion, full of sharp pebbles and deep well-like ruts, where the effluent-filled drains reeked, lived a handful of other ancient Brahmins. They could trace their great, great, great grandfathers who had lived in the same mediaeval houses up to seven generations, hence they were proud to recall their association with the distant past and congested narrow alley. To a much-travelled person it might have been a matter of great regret that the head of households had seen nothing of the world outside, and some had never been as far as the city, but to the Brahmins it was a matter of great pride to recount the years they and their forefathers had spent in the crumbling houses. In fact, sometimes it would become a kind of competition between families to establish that their forefathers had not set foot out of the village for up to six, seven generations or as many centuries. These Brahmin families were now materially poorer than the landowners and the only relic of their past pride was their spiritual ascendancy over other races, their purity of blood and distinguished births. However, people's attitudes were changing and they were gradually losing their status and position of nobility. Their sources of income had dried up too, since the Sikhs started having their own priests to conduct their ceremonies. Now the Brahmin fortunes were dwindling fast. They stood at the crossroads of a new society and made themselves an enigma – an oddity. There were only two courses left for them. One was to completely abandon their conditioning, which could be achieved by intermarrying into other races and castes or, secondly, to have sufficient economic means to carry on with the same stubbornness. In a predominantly Sikh village they occupied marginal positions; they were often ignored and insulted but they still continued to uphold the view that Sikhism was really a branch, part and parcel of Hinduism, but they dared not openly convey this message to the Sikhs who were already sick of their bigotry and general intolerance. So, inwardly, they saw themselves as set apart from the Sikhs and huddled in the security of their own little clique. But when in front of an aggressive Sikh who could outmanoeuvre them, they had learnt to become humbler, sweeter, mellower and to ply him with suitable eulogies and epithets.

In their masculine Brahmin society, women had no place; they were often shut away in the dark, stifling rooms where they spent most of their lives doing slavish chores or procreating like blind bats, ill-fed and ill-clothed. Even in these conditions they never forgot that they were the chosen few to whom God had spoken and was especially kind for their past Karma, and that birth in a Brahmin family was indeed unattainable and they were the privileged few, even if they were illiterate and could not read a word of the *Bhagvad Gita* or the *Ramayana*, even though they starved because they refused to do manual work and had little to subsist on.

Next door to Grandma Palika's ancient house, in a one-roomed hovel, lived an aged widow called 'Chandi' Brahmini. Her real name was not Chandi but, being of a very vile temper, shouting abuse and cursing all the time, she was called, 'Chandi' the Goddess of Wrath. She was a frail-looking, tall, sallow woman who liked to align herself with Grandma Palika, often managing to squeeze a meal or two out of her, but she would soon fall from Grandma Palika's esteem and be obliged to go from door to door blessing people and getting food in return. She had one son and thirteen grandsons with whom, in the beginning, Chandi went to stay. But the daughter-in-law soon grew weary of Chandi's temper, so Chandi moved away to spend the rest of her days cursing and swearing at her son with his 'no good' wife and that army of rats, her sons. Chandi also loved to gossip: news travelled faster with her than the local post office. Grandma Palika was one of those people who pretended that they had no ears for idle rumour, and although she never actually encouraged Chandi to give her the latest news, nevertheless she managed to obtain the vital parts of most new stories. Whenever anyone saw Chandi examining the sky or looking at her toenails, those people who got wise to her knew she was eavesdropping.

On the other side of Grandma's house was a kind of vacant shop. It had a door made out of solid iron bars with a huge padlock attached to it. In this place 'Mad Hari' was shut up day and night. He would come to the door, clutch at the bars, shout, snarl and bare his teeth at Asha. He always called everyone by the name 'Juggi'. It seemed that he could not recognise anyone but Juggi, and he was totally taken over with a self-consuming hatred for him. His abuse was so vile and frightening that people fled as they came by his cell. Only some adolescents and layabouts came to watch him, listen to his abuse and chuckle at Mad Hari's bawdy and lewd expressions, and particularly when he shouted again and again, 'Juggi, I shall fuck with your daughter yet. I will strip her and fuck her, and fuck her, and fuck her.'

They say that Mad Hari was once not mad. In fact he was a handsome figure of a young man. He, being the only son, was married to a very pretty girl when quite young, and of this marriage he had the most beautiful, doe-eyed gentle daughter called Kamla. But Hari did not love his wife and instead he had a turbulent affair with Juggi's eldest daughter who, though plain, was cherished and indulged by him. He gave her all his wife's gold jewellery and silk sarees, and openly admitted to his friends that he had a sexual relationship with her. When the rumours reached Juggi he was livid with anger. Not only did he marry his daughter off immediately but he also wanted to ensure that Hari was a broken man. He was a rich man and being in cahoots with the village nobility could do anything. So he visited the local police station, bribed the Thanedar (officer-in-charge) and got Hari a trumped up record and charged with being a vagabond of the first order. After this episode, Mad Hari was imprisoned time after time for crimes he did not commit and was brutally beaten up till every little bone in his body broke. After some years of this treatment Hari went mad. Everyone referred to him as Mad Hari and later he was put in his barred cell. There he sat, crouched all day, howling with rage like a mad dog. His tongue used to hang, his huge red eyes used to roll about and he used to froth at his mouth. Children dreaded him and would not dare pass in front of his door but when they did they forgot their fear and watched the dog-like man, fascinated, till the fear got the better of them and they ran screaming to their mothers. Mad Hari ate his food from the floor. He would chew and lap up food like a dog, never using his hands, making growling noises.

On the opposite side of the cell stood a red-brick house. Here lived the 'Babu', as he was called by everyone, with his wife. Babu was a Brahmin astrologer. He was lean and tall, with a very straight back and curled his moustaches with great patience. He also used to put eye liner in his eyes to accentuate their brilliance and redness. He wore dazzling white clothes and carried himself with great dignity. He did nothing else but tell fortunes – and make a fortune. But all his knowledge about the stars and the future was a confidence trick. Those who remembered his origins could tell that he came from a poor background. His father was barely literate, and he did not bother to pass even this skill on to his son who largely grew up on the streets. Babu became a master of human nature and knew all about human behaviour and could easily satisfy his customers by telling them what they wanted to hear. Soon his reputation spread to the neighbouring villages, so that he was never short of customers who wished to have their fortune told. Some of them would travel as far as twenty miles and would stand humbly outside his sitting room with dusty shoes in their hands, pouring with sweat because of the intense heat, but he would be in no hurry to usher them in. He would go on taking his time, mumbling Shalokas from the *Gita* haphazardly and tying the knot of his dhoti. Then he would climb a high wooden dais, put the sacred thread over his ear, open his big Almanac, and sit down cross-legged, submerged in holy thoughts.

Presently his wife would open the door and let the party in, and he would begin in a semi-hypnotic tone, 'You are not happy. Your life is full of sorrow. It is the sun that is after you, and Saturn is following close behind.' The clients were grateful and wondered how the all-knowing Babu could put his finger so precisely on all their problems, troubles and misfortunes. His life was full of false rituals and ceremonies. After prayers he would go upstairs and water the Sun God most reverently, as if this all-pervading God was dying of thirst. Neither would he allow himself an interview with a person on his first visit. He would sit upstairs and secretly watch his wife tell the weary traveller that he was away and to come back again another day. Many a time people arrived bewildered and confused with sick and dying children, but he never told them that he could not cure their sickness, and occasionally a child would die on his doorstep during his mumbling about Shri Krishna and while he was preparing the charms and amulets. In fact he was often heard to boast that he never sent anyone away who came in the name of God. But his life's pretence continued and he seemed to flourish in his practice. He had everything in plenty but no children. He maintained that he could cure other people's children yet he failed to save his own eleven who all died in infancy. This did not seem to affect him but his wife was left chronically sick. She had pulmonary tuberculosis and he could not cure her either. She was a shrivelled-up, thin, monkey-like female with a bent back who worked hard, doubled up, despite her ill-health. But after every task such as washing clothes or cleaning, she would cough and vomit blood in the drain which ran in the middle of the street. She continued coughing and spitting, spitting and coughing, infecting little children and young women who flocked freely to listen to her gossip and who also enjoyed the sweets she was generously showered with by her husband's congregation.

The Babu woman had little companionship or solace from her husband. She had an obsession for human company and would many a time snatch upon Asha's arm with shrivelled up, claw-like fingers and, with her little shrunken eyes, implore her to sit down a while with her. But Asha dreaded the woman and her frightening, choking cough, so she tried to rush away from her and would hold her breath till she was past the big ugly house.

Next door to Babu's house in a little mud hut lived a thin, tall, dark, gipsy-like woman. She was married to a short, fat, stump-legged man who was perpetually out of work. The pair looked very comical when they stood together because of their odd shapes and sizes. The man was pint-sized and the woman, in comparison, appeared to be a giant. He always wore big boots on his little round feet and ran about with quick, short steps like one of the dwarfs from Hansel and Gretel. Sometimes the woman would put the man's shirt on and it would only reach her belly button so everyone in the street would have a good laugh at their expense. Her husband, though out of work, was very fond of eating well and would spend most of the day planning what he was going to eat. They were only a young couple who had already gathered four children and did not get on well with each other. They had loud rows, and people would creep towards the house to listen and laugh. The man's most common address for the woman was 'you bitch', and she always used to answer back 'you dog'. Yet they carried on in acrimony because divorce was unthinkable. Then one day Asha found the woman sobbing and beating her breasts. Asha wanted to know what was upsetting her so desperately. It was the same old story – the woman was pregnant again and there was not enough food in the house for all of them.

Asha found the depth of her pain unimaginable. It seemed to envelop her from head to toe: her eyes had become very dull and they were circled with dark black rings as if she had been crying all night. Asha had never seen so much despair and the woman's pain moved her very much. She now openly cursed her husband for thrusting more motherhood on her when there was not enough food to feed, nor clothes to cover them. The man sat there shamefaced and kept on repeating, 'Well, this is married life. You can't help it, can you, now? This is the law of nature, a man can't help nature.' But the woman kept shouting at him in derisory tones, 'You fat, little mongrel. You got your chance that night! How could I have pushed you away without making a noise when the children were asleep beside me. Look what you have done to me now.' And she continued to shout and sob bitterly.

Asha could not fully understand the tension or the nature of the woman's worries but she understood and saw that they were profound, profound enough to make a big, strong, capable woman shake with misery. Later she tried to give herself a miscarriage but failed. Then she begged Asha to escort her to the dispensary nurse because she was very sick. Asha assumed that she was ill but when they went there together she begged the nurse to abort her and offered to pay her twenty rupees. The nurse told her that she was a 'respectable' married woman with young children and did not undertake such illegal work. She also frightened her by saying that she could bleed to death and that she could also go to prison. The tall woman was still determined and told her that she could sell her jewellery if she would help. Gradually she resigned herself to her fate and produced the fifth child – a daughter. Asha went to see her immediately after the birth where the woman lay in a dark room.

141

Her weeping, swollen face could barely be seen, and beside her sat the village sweeper biting her unclean nails and at the same time bathing the little girl in a jugful of not too clean water. Her shalwar was still stained with blood and her bottom lip was bloodstained too; she had bitten it to stop making a noise. In one corner of the room an old woman was digging a hole to bury the placenta. While all this activity went on inside, in the outer room sat her husband, wondering what to eat that day.

The oppression and gossip at Sarē Marē had become too much for Malika. She was looking for an outlet. It came in the shape of a full-page advertisement in the city paper. They were recruiting Indian staff in British hospitals. She had always wanted to take up medicine and now was her chance. She applied to a hospital in Birmingham. She was accepted to train as a nurse, with accommodation provided and fares paid. It was the beginning of a new life away from restrictions – her entry into a free society.

Malika's departure gave the family a great jolt. Malika had done everything in the house: she had managed money; she shopped; she looked after the younger children; and she ran the household very ably. She had developed an indispensable role for herself and was more of a mother to her siblings than the mother who was either busy looking after the cattle or cooking. Malika attended to them when they were sick, washed and combed their hair and made all their clothes. But along with these favours she was a hard taskmaster with a terrible temper. It was she who instilled discipline and etiquette in her sisters. She had a habit of twisting Asha's ears until tears ran from her eyes; she also pulled her hair or simply gave her a hard slap on the face – all painful judgements of her wrath. The parents had given her complete freedom to exercise this right and, being the eldest, she demanded respect. She was never called by her first name by the sisters, and despite enduring many painful beatings from her they never harboured any ill-will towards her for that was an accepted role.

When she left, she took away her flamboyance, her music, her laughter and her vivacious mannerisms. The house now appeared empty, dull and quiet. Many of the village women, who used to come to Malika for a massage, eye drops and many other female ailments stopped coming. Or they would remark, 'Your sister used to be so wise, she had the looks and the wisdom; you may have the brains but not her healing powers!' The family waited earnestly for her long, comprehensive letters, giving minute details of life in The Midlands.

Gradually the balance of power began to re-establish itself. The mother did not change her role but became more traditional in her outlook concerning her other two daughters. Shanta now had the keys for the money and valuables but she was always too serious, conservative and puritanical. She resented flippancy and light-heartedness and somehow the mother listened to her talk and agreed with her. Suddenly, new and irksome regulations came into play. The girls were not allowed to go for walks and Asha felt it most of all. She was not allowed to go to the shops, talk to any boys or uncover her head.

Shanta was determined that no one should have cause to talk about the family even if it meant the stifling and sudden death of their embryonic adolescence. Soon the upstairs windows had new shutters and blinds hung on them. Not only did the blinds hang but they were also tied securely with ribbons so that they could not be moved aside to peep out – even the wind could not move them. All the bright clothes were put away and, in their place, white homespun, coarse shalwars and kameez had to be worn. Asha's mother had already complained that Asha looked too eagerly at herself in the mirror and that, while walking, she looked at her clothes admiringly and smiled to herself. She insisted that Asha curb her loud laughter because it attracted attention; she must always look at the floor while out walking; she must always cover her bust and hair with her duppatta, although she had hardly any bust; she must not wear any glass bangles or jewellery of any kind.

This was indeed a very strange family reaction to Malika's absence. Had they now given in to village pressures? Would the rules be changed in relation to Asha? Used as Asha was to nomadic wanderings from her childhood, she found the transition too stifling and painful to cope with. Most of the time she was fed on English literature which upheld rebellion, freedom, individualism and free will. Asha yearned for freedom and yet her life was shackled. She had been used to running about in the wheat and sugar cane fields, singing to the skies and the trees. Her mother had little idea why she gave up trying to communicate, shut herself away in the world of books and even stopped eating. At the same time she had a real admiration for her grandmother's and mother's stoical, hard-working lives. They worked like slaves and both accepted pain and sorrow as part of life. She would have liked to cry and scream if she was unhappy, and she wished to reach hard for happiness. Could she ever become like them? Grandma Palika was like an ancient tree which, though sparse of leaves and graceful limbs, still retains that quality which suddenly makes one seem foolish and insignificant in its presence. Though Grandma Palika was not a literate person it was difficult to question and argue about her ways. She had the experience. Her normal answer was, 'Shut up, child, what do you know about anything? You have to live four score years before you can question my ways.' This reply, though short in logic, was quite effective in achieving its aims. Grandma was also poetic in her vision, and used similes and metaphors to describe her old age. She would often talk in a half-singing tone, 'I am an aged tree by the river bank, much battered by the sun, wind, hail and rain. My feet are fast eroded by the action of the waves and, one day soon, I shall be uprooted and blown away. And there shall I rot and be eaten by ants, worms and beetles till God calls me and I go forth to await his further orders.'

The image of her God was never gentle and loving. Her God was high-handed, cruel and revengeful. She always classified herself a 'Sinner', ever ready and waiting for her justly deserved suffering and punishment from God for her misdeeds. Grandma always called him a Just God but his justice appeared to be very severe indeed when Asha looked at her repentant and suffering Grandmother. But Grandma also had faith in the inevitable and resigned herself to the treatment God would mete out to her.

There were days when Grandma Palika became very quiet and thoughtful; she felt that her debt to God was still outstanding and though she had been to all the Tiraths (pilgrimages) in the North and the South, she had a craving to visit the Great Mother Ganges again before she breathed her last. So, on some days, she would become very introspective and sigh, uttering the name of Rama and Krishna alternately, and confiding in Asha that her end was very near.

Now Grandma Palika was not a feeble woman, and she knew very well that she could last another ten to twenty years but as she said, 'You never know about the "running vehicle", it may break down at any time!' Asha's mother was another pious devotee of the river Ganges, 'Mother Ganga', as they called it. She planned a holy journey with Grandma Palika; she also included her youngest son Vijay in the itinerary to be sanctified in the sacred river for the first time in his life. Grandma Palika collected all her savings which were further generously supplemented by the daughter-in-law. The granddaughter Asha, now an educated girl of sixteen, hoped to escort them on the trip and see to all their complicated needs, diet, prayers and visits. The date was set as the 1st of August in the month of the full moon (Purnima) and the monsoons. Then the river was full and flowed rapidly; its water leaped to the sky in the inner turmoil of rushing, gushing, mountain rivulets, and its clear waters were turned into a mud-swelled, sandy-red colour. It was when the new waters came and the river was made holier than ever that a dip in its dark waters made the pilgrims the purest from the soles of their feet to their innermost souls.

They had baked some savoury parathas, stuffed with little fried brown onions and sweet new potatoes. They also carried tamarind sauce as an accompaniment and semolina pudding for afters and a variety of vegetable curries, peppers and green beans, okra and the acrid karelas and heaps of pickles and jams. They also had packed rations for their stay: tins of clarified butter, flour, sugar, tea and any other thing they would need on the journey and during their stay. Grandma had tied everything neatly in little bundles and she carried the cooked food in brass containers which were covered with hessian squares.

She wanted the minimum amount of clothing to be carried so that she could carry the largest number of containers back full of sacred river water. She had requests from all over the village for water and also for little keepsakes from the sacred city of Haridwar. During the journey she carried a walking stick and also refused to wear any shoes. Vijay was dressed in a blue shirt and matching shorts and wore a red velvet hat with a blue tassel on it. Mother had a white muslin saree on and Grandmother wore the *Shalwar Kameez* of her own spun khadi, woven in the village and sewn by herself. Her shalwar fitted tightly around her ankles, her kameez hung loose and her duppatta was starched white. Despite her age her step was light and joyous while the bundles and bottles banged and clattered and made an embarrassingly noticeable din. The journey was long and weary, and the sand and dust blew into their eyes. The fields seemed scorched brown and very dry. The farmers were digging and cutting new channels in case it rained but the rains were already delayed and there were no clouds in sight. The party's enthusiasm had already ebbed when they reached the village station. Vijay was crying for iced water but the pitchers on the platform were all empty. There was no shade in sight and the train was late. Asha deposited the suitcases and bundles on a burning hot wooden bench and asked her mother and grandmother to wait while she went to buy five Anna third class tickets for everyone. These would take them to the nearest city on the first leg of their journey.

This was the first time that Asha considered she was doing a responsible job and going so far away unescorted by a male and being in charge of two old women and a child. She felt her heart jump with pride and power and hot blood rush to her cheeks at the thought of numerous brave adventures she might encounter and deeds of heroism she might be able to perform. She imagined she saw a hundred gangsters, one thousand layabouts and vagabonds and, with one sweeping gesture of her hand, she dismissed them all. While she stood deliciously daydreaming, forgetting the mission she had come upon, the station master grew weary and restless so she awoke from her visions and looked for the purse sewn in a hidden pocket in her vest under her jumper. The train was late but at least it came and they scrambled in. As usual the train was full of Jats (farmers) who occupied all the seats, the standing places, the steps and the doors, the door handles and snored and snorted. Some even occupied the luggage racks; they lay in a huddled, death-like torpor, never rising, never waking, and never making any room for others. Gradually, Grandma Palika shuffled and crept sideways like a crab, secured herself a small space next to the lavatory, and sat herself down with her luggage resting all around her in ill-assorted bundles. Jaya found room on a linseed sack and she squatted herself down with Vijay on her lap. As usual in her friendly fashion she immediately started a conversation with a Harijan woman who squatted next to her on her haunches holding an unwashed, naked child to her breast. Later she forgot to push the breast back in her Kameez and it kept dangling about in total unselfconsciousness. Some youths in one corner joked and sniggered about the woman's breast, and the child started sucking it again and then bit it. This made the woman conscious of her uncovered breast. She first slapped the child's bottom who yelled, and then she pushed the breast back in her kameez with a short apologetic laugh. Grandma, in her corner, sneered and made faces at Jaya talking to everyone, and then she went back to sleep.

Later the youths turned their attention to Asha and whistled at her, and started talking in loud, artificial voices to attract her attention, but Asha kept on tying and untying a hanky around her wristwatch. She wanted the bystanders to be aware of her watch and the best way to attract their attention was to play nonchalantly with its strap until it was noticed. Though it was an old watch which never kept good time and had been discarded by both her elder sisters, she treasured it. Asha looked out of the train window and saw the burnt, cinnamon-coloured fields and trees covered with wild berries flying past. She saw herds of buffalo, staring indifferently at the train hurrying, huffing and puffing. She saw groups of expectant, ill-clad, open-mouthed village children, and she was proud that she was inside the train and not on the other side. She was almost as proud as if she was the owner of the train. At the next station the college boys alighted to roam about, display their fine clothes and walk lazily, and then step back on, very coolly, sure footed, aloof and unconcerned when the train was already in motion.

By now Asha's eyes were sore and aching with particles of coal from the engine. Suddenly, the atmosphere in the carriage grew tense and an uproar could be heard in the distance. Everyone gathered up and clutched his luggage. They had reached the city. And their long journey had begun in earnest.

Through a maze of shunting engines, puffing, hissing and whistling trains, they reached the platform. Everyone seemed to be in a hurry and the porters with their red shirts and brass plates gleaming in the sun ran noisily. Heaps of stallholders crowded the platforms and cried themselves hoarse selling their goods. They walked gingerly through the vast crowds and Asha demurely pushed her hand deeper into her vest pocket to get some money for tickets to Dehra Dun. They had to wait four hours for the next train, and when it arrived it was spilling with human beings, who sprawled, squeezed and bundled themselves all over it and every inch of available space was taken. Most of them were going to visit the shrines of the Seven Mothers and would alight half way. Jaya managed to secure a seat for all of them though Asha had to sit on her squatting grandmother, and Vijay in his mother's lap like a baby. There was a deserter from the army in one corner of the carriage; he was in handcuffs and was being taken for disciplinary procedures and court martial but the man was indignant and kept on shouting filthy abuse at the Government and its accomplices. There were also some holy men, scantily dressed, their hair matted and crawling with lice which they did not wish to kill. Asha was indignant: it was horrible to see such nakedness and filth going around in the name of religion, but her mother was quietly amused and accepting. A hawker came aboard to sell medicine for deficient sight but he himself appeared to be blind. The train passed through different cities and towns and the Punjab seemed to be one vast, never-ending tract of green and brown fields, lush forests and rivers. Then came Himachal with its beautiful curtain of greenery and the vast Himalayas kept looming larger and larger. The train passed through narrow tunnels, deeply cut through the hillsides, by the paddy fields and dense jungles and undergrowth of the foothills, and after two long days they faced Dehra Dun. It was disappointing for Asha for with a name as beautiful as that it turned out to be a dirty, crowded city. Everyone seemed to be running and a glass of milk cost three times the amount it cost at home. They went to visit a Sikh Gurudwara which was decorated with the stuffed heads of stags, and Grandma Palika, with her usual broadmindedness, took part in the prayers and was given a lump of sweet, greasy halwa for the blessings which she insisted on sharing with everyone. Asha and Vijay felt very tired and dirty with all the coal dust from the steam train but the Sikh priest would not allow them to wash their face and hands with soap.

Here, a minor catastrophe took place. Asha lost the address of the cousin they were going to stay with. There was a great deal of trouble and turmoil and Grandma Palika blamed herself for trusting a 'halfwit' like Asha. Then she discovered that the key for the suitcase was also missing, along with her hand-towel. The only course now open to them was to catch the next train to Haridwar, their next stop in the holy pilgrimage, and be at the sacred feet of Mother Ganga. Late in the evening, tired and weary, they entered the strange city and started looking for the Dharamshalla (religious rest house) where a room was already earmarked for them as it had been built for charity by one of Grandmother's cousins. Eventually they found it, not far from the station. Its big wooden doors were closed, but they stepped in through a narrow entrance in the wall and entered a spacious courtyard planted with mangoes and flowering trees. Through this courtyard of paving stones and trees they reached a flight of stairs which connected various storeys of the rambling building. The place was full of cooking smells and thronged with people.

As they stepped inside a tiny, narrow, rather shabby room, Grandma Palika said that they had entered the Gates of Heaven, but Asha felt that Heaven would never have been able to reside in that dingy, narrow room. It had a tatty rope bed in it and nothing else except swarms of mosquitoes. Outside, the monkeys sat in large family clusters and jumped about like rubber balls on the roof; soon they ambled inside and stole the rice and tore their clothes and when

Grandma shouted, made faces at her. They even rushed menacingly to hit her, and Grandma had to wave her walking stick about.

'Where is my bed?' shouted a red-eyed, balding, God-seeking misery of an old ascetic in orange robes. His eyes were blood red and he seemed to have been drinking ground cannabis juice. 'How dare you move my bed?' he demanded. Mother was most apologetic; with her hands folded she proceeded, 'Sorry, Baba Ji, the child had a raging fever and needed some sleep, and you were out.' She humbly pointed to the sleeping Vijay who was suffering from heat and exhaustion. 'Don't Baba Ji me, you Old Woman, just bring us that bed out! he demanded. Oh, the agony and the humiliation of seeing a weary little woman dragging a hefty bed out, and that big rascal of a holy man, glowering and then smiling to himself and looking pious! 'You stupid idiot, you devil, God hasn't ever touched you, God has never come your way, and never will,' thought Asha looking at him rudely and defiantly.

The night of the full moon and I, weary and longing, longing for something I had lost. Longing for the lost hours, lost in the darkness of the hills and plains! Mother does not care to comb her hair. Grandma and she are fasting, fasting to please the Gods, fasting for their sins to be forgiven, the sins they don't even know about but believe they have committed. The sins that are there now in their thoughts, in their ignorant minds, or perhaps they are all lost souls, groping. Groping in the dark to comprehend something I don't know about, something substantive, something concrete. If they possessed the touch and the sensitivity of a blind man they then might feel their sins.

Asha felt that both her Grandmother and her mother's lives were controlled by some hidden, dark force which was magical and evil at the same time. This strange force had given them some pain and numerous sorrows to live with so that they could atone for them. Mother is now faint with hunger and she buys a ball of sweet rice and goes to a tap to wash her hands and rinse her mouth of all the sins in this holy city. And there comes a monkey, creeping, tiptoeing lightly, just like a burglar or a pickpocket, and with alacrity and nimbleness he picks up mother's rice ball and flees with it. Mother laughs feebly and says, 'Oh well, someone is eating it!' But Grandma says most emphatically, 'God be thanked, he sent his messenger down, the Holy Hanuman God, to accept his offerings.'

'But Grandma, mother needed it herself. She is very hungry.' And mother bravely totters home, feeble and bad-tempered through lack of food.

In the fast-flowing, murky river, Great Ganga, we have a daily dip. And the temple bells, they ring, they make a terrible noise, big enough to drown the river, to drive the people crazy and deaf. The city of temples booms; the statues, the stones loom large everywhere I turn. Huge vermilion-covered figures of the Monkey God Hanuman face me at every corner, and then there is the Temple of the Great Satee where the flame burns forever. To me this is a frightening place with many figures moving towards me all the time, creeping through the darkness of the temple vault and ready to wring my neck because I do not believe! I am frightened of my rebellious, unholy thoughts and am wondering if I am a sinner, and whether the Gods will pounce in a flash and punish me. And the bells still keep on clanging until my head feels bloated and achey.

Early one morning we walked barefoot on the dirty pavements, on Grandma's wishes that this should be so in the holy city. We saw hordes of beggars: some were blind and some were limbless; some were literally rotting. Some were freaks with monster heads, two heads, no nose, thalidomide-type deformities and many other freakish acts of nature. They were all rejected by humanity. Their cries, their shapes and their terrible pain haunted me in my sleep. They sat on pavements: those who could ran crying; the others were tottering, shuffling and crawling on all fours on their bottoms. There they were in the flower-strewn streets where stone Gods were worshipped.

The city was trying to put on a joyous air. The flower girls were selling flowers everywhere, sweet jasmine, gulmohar, mimosa, champak and the sweet buds of flame trees. The flowers were dew-covered, fresh and sweet, honey-scented, and some girls sold coconuts for few paisas. The crowds and swarms of people came and bought these and went to the river to float their offerings. The despairing beggars looked on with sunken eyes and observed it all. Why did they not scream at the contradictions – can hungry stomachs be ignored to feed the fat fish and worship the murky waters of river in turmoil? People turned their backs on them and ran away hurriedly. They were an unpleasant sight, to be shooed away like dogs. They were unclean and therefore punished by God for their past, invisible sins. But God, who is the father of us all, how could he ignore their need, and be cruel to them, and this, too, in the holy city?

On one side of the river bank people were busy feeding the fish; on the other were rows of beggars patiently holding out their empty bowls to be filled. Somebody would occasionally throw a paisa in their direction and they would fight with the venom of mad dogs. Even the ones at death's door revived momentarily. In the city of the Gods a sweet odour of incense rose heavenwards all the time. The tons of flowers were sweet and fragrant, and on the other side of the road were rows of beggars crying eternally in pain. 'Don't look that way, child, look at the beautiful river. Look how the flower petals and the coconuts make its waters colourful, sweet and scented. Drink the amrit (nectar), child, for who knows if you will ever come back to it again!'

Millions of people undressed and bathed in the muddy, murky waters. Millions of people were praying for their Mukti and millions of them were crying in fear in case they were refused. Millions of heads bobbed up and down searching for God and salvation in the Ganges. Some women were bathing with their husbands so that they could be blessed with happiness and their wishes granted. Others were praying, sitting and squatting on the wet Ghats with wet sarees clinging to their bodies, and their breasts and the pubic hair clearly visible to all. Some sat on the top steps lost in prayer while aimless youths tried to identify how many women were showing their private parts. Most had hair and armpits covered in sand and mouths full of grit, and the water of the river tasted, acrid, bitter, unpleasant and dirty.

'Mother, Vijay has peed in the river again!'

'Oh, you foolish boy, Ganga Mata will chastise you. It will make your penis rot,' says Grandma. Vijay begins to cry but the poor boy cannot help the sight of water, it makes him pee straightaway.

Grandma goes for a long walk and catches sight of the river in a lonely spot. She wishes at least to have a sip of the holy waters, and she tumbles and slides in the river, and if the boatmen had not rushed to rescue her she would have drowned. But she is stubborn and walks for miles all over the place and insists on bathing everywhere in public and crowded places. She has a religious madness just for a dip in the river. And I am bewildered and homesick and feeling lonely in this crowded city. All the Sadhus at the Ashram are hypocritical phoneys or misguided souls. They say they have nothing to do with worldly possessions, yet if you offer them money they readily offer you the black gourd they carry to keep the money in. They insist that their lives are holy and they keep away from women, yet they look at me in a most staring fashion.

A Sadhu in his thirties with a clipped head like a melon came and sat near Asha. He wore the usual vermilion robes and was grieved to know that she was a sceptic. He told her that the end of the world was near and the God of Death, the mighty Shiva, was ready to appear. 'You will see him riding a black horse with two sabres in his hands, and he is going to slay all the wicked ones including you.' He said it was written so in his books but Asha told him that his Death God needed something more potent than the sabres in this age of nuclear weapons. Upon hearing this sarcastic comment he grew sullen and walked away. But Asha knew he was interested in her and he kept coming back and asking her to accompany him to his room and see his collection of books. She followed him into a poorly lit room for she was a curious young girl and wished to know what was in his mind. After showing Asha a few old battered books on Hindu mythology he offered her a seat and sat beside her. He appeared tense, his breathing became faster and his little beady eyes kept seeking Asha's and giving her beseeching looks. He also kept mumbling that her limbs were made of silk and her eyes were those of the Lotus Goddess full of depth and understanding. Luckily for her, her mother called her before he had a chance to enhance his acquaintance, and afterwards she was wise enough never to give him the opportunity again.

Grandma Palika said that Bhooma Nand was a learned man and that we must ask him to visit the village, and mother seconded the proposal; all the time Bhooma Nand hovered like a fly around Asha. He kept on beseeching and imploring her to remind her mother to invite him to their house, and he would perform the best Havana and prayers they had ever had. He carried their luggage to the train on the day of departure and bit Asha's hand in desperation as the train pulled out. Asha kept on wondering whether God specifically chose him, his city and the river. But her heart said no, this was not so. Perhaps God was everywhere and nowhere, and that people were lost souls who could not find themselves. It rained hard all night and when they reached the village station, the roads were all flooded and the village of Sarē Marē looked like one vast lake with submerged fields and floating houses.

Grandma Palika squatted in her little room with a rosary in her hands, which trembled and shivered with cold. The light from the little earthen lamp fell in a dim circle around her and the big, wooden, oil-black beams in the ceiling looked like monstrous, age-old dinosaurs and dragons clinging to the ceiling. It was the middle of a wintry, cold night and Grandma sat huddled in a quilt, praying. Her thin lips opened and shut with rhythmic murmuring and kept pace with the running of the night. Presently she stopped, put her rosary away in an alcove and blew at the light which quivered and jerked weakly and then went out without much resistance. Grandma Palika was a lonely old widow of great age and, as she lay in bed, years passed before her mind's eye.

'This is the very room where I spent my first married night. I was young but remember it because your grandfather kept pinching me during the night, and I did not like him one bit, and wished the young man would go away. In the end, I scratched his face and bit his finger and he slapped me. Oh yes, I was completely ignorant then, not like you, nowadays, who know about everything and there's nothing left to know. Your grandfather, I must tell you, was a kind man, a good man. He was a big, dark man, with broad shoulders; he was built like a horse and of course he rode horses and had the most excellent saddle and he was very generous! He owned the finest race horses in the district, and whenever he bet it was a generous bet. Even when he lost heavily, he kept his word and honoured all his debts. Of course, in those days, we were very prosperous. Why, we owned the village and were the first people to build our houses on the land. Don't ask me where we came from but there have always been Palikas in Sarē Marē. Yes, your grandfather lost his father when he was a tiny babe, and the rest of the Palikas were after his life for the sake of his fortune, till one day his mother ran away with him to her own home. He grew up to be a man there, but remember, she came back to Sarē Marē as soon as he was big enough to look after his own. His mother was a good woman. She was very stubborn, strong-minded and wilful like all the Palika women, but she was also absolutely truthful. I have yet to meet anyone who could challenge her word. Your grandfather was a real gentleman, and I have known that every November at Deewali he fed the whole village at his doorstep. Well, this house has memories for me and that's why I would like to spend my last days here in peace. It is lonely here and very quiet, but it gives me time to think about my past sins and repent.

When I was fourteen I had my first child. It was a girl and I found myself very angry at being burdened with her. There was no time to look after a child and nobody told me how. I had to spin, grind, cook for thirteen people, scrub floors and clean all the brass pots and pans. It was no life for me, never mind a young child. Nobody was bothered about her – she was a girl. Well, I just wrapped her in a piece of cloth as if she were a little rag doll, and put her away, neatly wrapped, under the ancient wooden cupboard you see there. There the poor little thing lay, and nobody picked her up to see how she was. I dared not look at her for three days until I remembered that I must do something for her.

I can still see her little face and closed eyes as if she were in a deep sleep, and it still torments me. I have visited all the holy places and the Tiraths on my bare feet until I am weary and blistered but there is no forgiveness for this sin – if only I had had more sense. Then I was only fourteen but I know that this sin shall drown me in the great river at the end. Don't make excuses for me, child, don't tell me it was ignorance or just an upset child's mind. No, it was a deliberate act of great sin, and I cannot ever forgive myself. There's a hole burnt right through my soul and I cannot ever forget it. That is the worst deed that I ever committed in my whole life and must wait for justice now, at the great Gates of the Almighty.'

'Grandma, don't cry. You are the best Grandma in the whole world, and I am very sad that this happened to you. You confess to me and I forgive you. Perhaps I am that girl.' But Grandmother composes herself and goes on.

'Despite all my weaknesses we are the best people in the village, the highest, the Brahmins. We are a very special part of God, that's why I am telling you this. Don't ever forget your past and your caste, and the superiority of your forefathers. We are the chosen people.'

Her grandmother's confession confused Asha. She had thought of her as strong and infallible but now to see her weeping helplessly and looking to Asha for strength made her realise that she had changed even in her grandmother's eyes. Great secrets of the heart could be confided to her. But things at home continued in the same old way. After her trip to the Great Ganges, the village seemed a phoney old place and she had nothing to do. She had finished her two-year Entrance course and was now waiting expectantly for something wonderful to happen. Her sister Shanta and her mother decided that they ought to arrange her marriage. A young teacher at her father's school was approached. He had no mother and lived with two unmarried sisters and an elderly father in a nearby town. Asha was escorted there by her mother on some half made-up excuse.

Everything in their little house was shabby and had an air of threadbare gentility; the sisters were silent and humorless and the young man himself appeared to be dull and lifeless. The sisters offered them some tea out of unused, dusty china cups especially reserved for guests, but everything in the house had a recurrent theme of meanness, and Asha was glad to get out into the fresh air.

Later, her mother scolded her for laughing too much. But Asha always giggled when she was nervous. Then her mother blurted out that she should be modest as they could be her in-laws. This made Asha choke with tears of rage and humiliation. How could her mother be hawking around with her on display as if she was a suitable exhibit? She did not openly cry but told her mother in no uncertain terms that if the family did try to arrange her marriage in that house she would run away.

She was so vehement in this declaration that her mother was taken aback. Asha felt even more bitter towards her father whom she thought of as an ally and here he was finding suitable marriage partners for her amongst his own staff. On her return she looked into her suitcase at what assets she had to cope with an independent life. There were her Matriculation and Entrance certificates, a lucky piece of marble, two cowrie shells, some ribbons, some rounded pieces of wood and some sheets of paper with poems scribbled on them. She threw away the lucky marble and pieces of wood – they had lost their magical qualities and their potency to protect – and sat for a long time in the growing dusk considering what was the best course to follow. Should she run away to the city? She knew no one there and clearly two certificates, although 'First Class', could hardly provide her with an escape route. But luckily for her, the family temporarily dropped the idea of an instant marriage.

It was a long, slow, empty summer and although Asha's unescorted wanderings were severely curtailed, nevertheless she took a chance in the cool evenings. That particular evening she felt claustrophobic and went out on her own. A programme of electrification was going on to modernise the village: trenches were being dug and electric poles were being erected without the aid of much sophisticated machinery. Young men worked and climbed on these sky-high poles with great agility like circus acrobats. One young man in a cockatoo-bright turban was hanging upside down just clinging to the post with his legs. When he saw Asha coming he whistled and ordered the young man standing underneath to 'bow to her most humbly'. This he himself proceeded to do with an exaggeratedly sweeping gesture of his arm, and then he touched his forehead with the fingers of his open hand in a most humble manner. Then he shouted aloud for Asha to hear, 'This is no ordinary girl going for a walk – this here is a very *special* lady. Bow to her Highness, I say to you bow to her,' and the man standing on the ground followed his instructions rather sheepishly. Asha was much flattered by this episode. These two young men seemed much more intriguing and interesting. She marvelled at their beautiful physique and their agility. So full of romantic notions was she, and so anxious for an experience, that she lived and relived the brief scene many times in her mind's eye.

The winter had set in. One sunny day as she was hanging the washing in the sun, Asha caught sight of a pink turban and a smiling face which appeared so alive and full of mischief, and the very large hazel eyes threw her a playful wink. She had seen that face somewhere before, oh yes, it was the man on the electricity pylon. So he had come to stay in the vacant house two doors down, and there was his friend cooking a meal in the courtyard. His eyes kept linking longingly with Asha's and there was so much mobility in his face. And as Asha looked on, spellbound, his expressions changed so quickly, from a very pleasant surprise, to pleasure, to disappointment, and so on.

She was mesmerised and stood there in rapt attention with a wet towel in her hand and the bucket full of washing still at her feet. She heard Shanta calling and she fled. This strange mime show continued whenever Theep (as she found out his name later) had the opportunity. He talked not with a voice but his whole body and in this he was singularly well versed, a master craftsman. He was rarely close enough to talk to her in an ordinary way, so he invented a whole vocabulary of alternative communication and another language which required the use of his hands, his face, his eyes, his head, and with these he could communicate the most complex of messages. Asha walked on air as he imparted to her his eternal love, and that he sent her his kisses, long and lingering, his tight hugs, his close embraces and his undying and desperate love.

When he walked down the street to carry water from the water pump Asha dropped him a love poem on scented paper which he picked up quickly enough and kissed, then carefully put it in his breast pocket next to his heart. Asha started spending interminable hours in front of the mirror, putting kohl in her dark eyes to accentuate their largeness, dressing herself more carefully and tying her hair in scarlet ribbons. She also spent hours in front of the upstairs window, waiting for him and drinking it all in. Theep, too, dressed flamboyantly. He wore bright check shirts and, as he had very long hair, bright-coloured turbans in bright flamingo pinks, oranges, aquamarines, purples and greens. Theep appeared to be a young man of indeterminate age, fair-skinned with a light-brown beard and a fine, chiselled nose. His eyes were fascinating and had the intensity and luminosity of the amber eyes of a tiger. These were the most impressive feature of an otherwise broad face with a narrow forehead. His gait was curiously ambling yet graceful; it was as if a camel was walking in the desert sands.

Initially Asha resisted his overtures, although she was driven to watch through great curiosity. Gradually his endearing antics grew on her impressionable child's mind and she became a participant and an actor in the drama. One day he entreated her to put make-up on her face, powder, rouge and lipstick. Asha did not have any of these but she did have a red pencil. This she dipped in water and rather painstakingly painted her face, and this exaggeratedly painted face, rather like that of a Pierrot doll, she proudly exhibited to him through the window. A hundred kisses and embraces flew in her direction and Theep did a little dance in the narrow, ugly courtyard. Unfortunately for Asha she was not the lone receiver of these gifts: Shanta and her mother watched this complex array of distance communication from the rooftop and, unlike Asha, they were disgusted and shocked. Later, they descended on Asha and observed her clownish face, but instead of thinking this to be a joke they were highly censorious.

They forbade Asha to go near the window; heavy bamboo blinds appeared and were firmly secured to the bars so that they could not be moved an inch either way. Asha's imprisonment and incarceration were now complete. She also got a severe lecture about the family honour. She tried to find alternatives to keep herself occupied. She missed Theep's distant company and his inventiveness and the complexities of the alternative, secret-coded, special language he had created for her alone and which she understood completely. She tried to replace the windows with the high-up, narrow, barred ventilators but all she could ever see were Theep's wide, sad eyes and the fuchsia turban. It was all too painful, so she gave up in despair and shut herself away in her solitary misery.

A week passed. A whole range of bewildering feelings charged Asha's mind and took hold of her psyche. Anger, guilt and desire overwhelmed her. Then one day, by chance, when she was not looking for him at all, she nearly bumped into him in the narrow alley, when no one was around. He whispered to her that he missed her, could not sleep a wink at night, and would she please meet him outside his house at 1 am that night. Asha tried to protest and make excuses, but he was gone. All day, she was filled with apprehension, foreboding and guilt. When she sat down to eat, she could not eat anything, and her mother looked at her inquiringly for a long time, then wanted to know if she was ill. Asha felt thoroughly wretched, worried and preoccupied. She wondered if the family knew her secret, and that night she wished to creep away like a thief to see Theep as that was her promise to him. She wondered if her face carried the secret, written all over her forehead, 'this girl is a little betrayer', but no one asked her any questions. But alas, she was so tired wrestling with her confusion and her desire that she did not wake up until the early morning. She was contrite and worried in case Theep thought that she had let him down. In the morning she offered to clean and wash down the upstairs drains and had the opportunity to talk to Theep who stood now in the courtyard with head bowed, utterly lost in gloom. She told him that she had overslept. When he grasped the meaning he laughed and, pointing to his watch and the sun, he told her to come at the same time that night.

When night came she lay wide awake. The rains had come so the beds were taken downstairs to the bedrooms and the verandah. Her bed was in the verandah and next to her slept her mother. When she crept away to meet Theep it would be a very daring act indeed, right under her mother's nose.

One o'clock came. Silently she got out of bed, surreptitiously tucked a pillow in her place and covered it with her beautiful quilt. From a distance it appeared as if she was sound asleep, all curled up like a sleeping child. She crept downstairs in the dark and marvelled at her audacity, her daring and became momentarily petrified at her own utter and complete wickedness. She unlocked the front door, removed the bolt and unhooked the chain from its catch stealthily – she did not dare lock the door on herself – and then stepped into the street. The street was dark but gradually forms began to appear, elongated shadows of trees, tall, spindly houses blanketing the street with darkness. Soon she had jumped over the wall and underneath it stood Theep ready to hold her in his arms if she should stumble or fall and carry her away into the night. He hugged her and she involuntarily shook in his embrace. He had a peculiar aroma around him, a mixture of musk and bitter almonds, and she buried her nose in his flannel shirt. They walked a bit before they reached his one-roomed, ground floor flat. The room was the first one to be electrified and was lit harshly with a powerful, naked lightbulb. Under this glaring light his face looked leathery, coarse, lined and old, and she could not tell how old he was. He looked unattractive, like a wizened monkey, rather than the dashing, youthful, handsome hero she carried in her visions daily. Their nearness to each other frightened her, made her self-conscious and tongue-tied. She had thought of so many questions to ask him, but the man she thought she knew over the past few months was now a remote stranger. He was clumsy and nervous in his movements and his breath smelt acrid and bitter as he tried to kiss her. He said that his family were refugees from Pakistan, from Majha, and that apart from an older brother and a sister-in-law he had no one to love; his parents had died during the partition riots and upheavals. He asked her if she had any previous experience with men but she was so visibly alarmed that he changed the subject and gently patted her cheek and held her chin lovingly with an index finger.

'You're only young,' he said, 'you will learn, I could teach you many things.' After some time in his company Asha felt awkward and became restless and frightened and wished to go back home. Theep looked out to see if the road was clear but outside stood

Asha's mother like Nemesis seeking revenge. He rushed in hurriedly and shut the door, suggesting that they should run away on his bike but this did not seem very practical. Asha decided that she had to return and face the consequences.

When she reached home it was early morning. Her family had lit a fire in the hearth and sat huddled around it. Her mother, her father, her younger brother and her sister. They all faced her with accusing eyes. 'Where have you been in the middle of the night?' her father demanded. Their faces now assumed a deep look of entreaty and earnestness as if they wanted her to give them an answer which would reassure them and dispel their worst fears. Her mother was hollow-cheeked and haggard; she kept licking her dry lips and twisting her duppatta. Her father's face haunted her most: it was a curious shade of green; his eyes were sunk deep into their sockets and he looked like a corpse. The rest were curious and expectant as a great melodrama was about to be unfolded. She registered each and every face and every movement at that moment, for was she not the supreme culprit? Her father broke the cold, still spell in the room and asked her, 'Where have you come from?' Asha could not bring herself to deceive them, she told him simply enough, 'I have been with Theep.' At this simple announcement her mother started weeping in a most disconsolate manner, beating her face and breasts and wailing. She was not prepared for the extent of her mother's grief nor her father's utter and absolute humiliation.

She looked at her sister and Vijay: in their eyes she was already a condemned and tainted person. She could not grasp the reality of what was happening to her; momentarily she thought she was sleepwalking and participating in a play conducted by the souls from the underworld. Her mother kept repeating. 'If only I had strangled you at your birth! I wouldn't have lived to see this evil day, daughter. You have destroyed our Izzat, and our family name, you are a visitation of revenge and an evil curse on the family.' Gradually, life came to her father. He moved resolutely and ordered everyone to bed.

The sun was up high when Asha awoke the next day. She hoped that last night's nightmare was a bad dream as she made her way downstairs, but one look at her mother's face, pale, haggard and crestfallen, covered with self-inflicted bruises, convinced her that it was not so. As usual she asked Vijay to share breakfast with her, but Vijay told her that she was wicked and that he was not allowed to speak to her. Food was disdainfully thrown at her as if she was a condemned criminal, and she refused to eat it. Her mother would not communicate with her and told her that to all intents and purposes she was now dead to her. But Shanta ordered her back to her bedroom and told her to stay there. The curtains were drawn all day in the room, and Asha slept and dreamt. She dreamt that people with axes and sticks were after her and that she was to be stoned until she died.

For two days and nights she lived in this nightmarish, twilight world where nothing seemed real and night and day merged and fused into one confusion. The family conferences went on downstairs while she was suspended in this grey world of drawn curtains and muffled sounds. Someone brought her food but she had little appetite and it stayed under her bed in many untouched bowls and plates. She could scarcely take in the course of events taking place around her and the way they affected her, so in this uncertain state she could hardly think of Theep. She hoped for his sake that he had gone away.

Late in the afternoon her father called in to see her. It was dark so a hurricane lamp was brought in and it now lay resting on the big wooden bedding box, making circles of eerie light. Her father appeared gentler and kinder as he put his arms around her and told her he still loved her. The forgiving side of his character contrasted so dramatically with the enormity of her own guilt and sinfulness that Asha started to cry and sob and ask for his forgiveness as she fell on his feet. He gently pulled her up and gave her his handkerchief and told her to wipe her eyes. Then he asked her in a harsh, solemn tone whether she had allowed Theep to 'take liberties with her' and whether she was still a virgin? 'Are you sure you won't bear a child?' he asked. This doubt and questioning cut Asha to the core of her soul. Her tears of repentance now choked her and stung her eyes; her great love and faith in her father assumed a question mark. She protested in a shocked and outraged voice, 'No father, I did no such thing!' But her mother had her doubts.

To her, visiting a man meant just one thing and it was no good taking endless baths to purify herself as her grandmother used to demand when she played with Harijan children. This time her soul was tainted; contact with a Sikh man in the middle of the night had reduced her to the lowest of the low and had turned her into an 'untouchable'. She was also told to pack her bags as her father intended to take her back to Sarē Dubē where, presently, her fate would be decided.

She threw the few things she had in a pillowcase, almost in a state of defiance now; she was being rejected; her mother was withholding her love, her charity, for forgiveness from her and her father was uncertain of her truthfulness. She was being sent away to quarantine, to see if she had got the 'dreaded disease', and she was tarnished overnight. If this was the test of love, they had failed unequivocally in Asha's eyes, and she was leaving home – an alienated stranger. Shanta did not say goodbye to her, Vijay only talked to her in the most perfunctory tones, and her mother had gone to bed with a severe headache. So Asha left with her pillowcase of possessions, an acute sense of loneliness in her heart and a profound ache at all her yesterdays. But she remembered to take with her a black and white picture of Theep which he had given her and which she kept hidden but worshipped like the holiest of deities; now perhaps she would have even more need for someone to be her God, her Shrine, the exalted image she could pay homage to and believe in, in her new total isolation and long loneliness.

The sameness of life at Sarē Dubē and carrying adult responsibilities for a girl of sixteen and a quarter needed getting used to. This time, her father chose not to live at the school house. Perhaps he had ample cause not to trust Asha in proximity to so many boys or perhaps he felt that he needed more room.

He rented the upper storey of a house. It had two little rooms upstairs, a courtyard and two open verandahs. As the place had been locked up for years, it was very dusty, overrun by ants, lizards and there were cobwebs everywhere. All the windows and doors were covered with layers and layers of dust; it was fine and powdery and went straight up one's nose, causing violent fits of sneezing. The walls and floors, once plastered with dung and mud, had now been eroded and were full of holes covered with wasps' and beetles' nests.

It was a laborious job for Asha to make the two rooms dust free, and pots and pans, chairs and beds dust free too. She had now come to accept her banishment with a grim stoicism and set out to make the house habitable. She plastered the walls and floors with a mixture of straw, mud and dung, and that abated the dust problem somewhat. Then she set out to shape a hearth for cooking out of bricks and clay. The house was at the end of a street whose inhabitants she did not know but gradually a lot of them grew curious at her living all alone with her father, and struck up friendships with her although she was always on her guard and maintained her distance.

The hardest job for her was to bring water in long zinc pails, first thing in the morning, from the well and to do all her father's and her own laundering by hand with cold water in the wintertime. The facilities in the house were primitive and she suffered from large, painful sores on her palms, knuckles and fingertips. Her father generally dressed in white. His clothes used to get grimy and grey as did the coarse towels and sheets. Asha took on all these roles of the little housekeeper without complaint.

It never occurred to her to question the judgement or the wisdom of her family who incarcerated her, banished her and put her away as an unwanted article. She was so near to them in distance and yet so distant in contact. During the first year of her stay in Sarē Dubē her father would disappear to Sarē Marē on Friday and come back on Monday, and during holidays her imprisonment in the dusty house was total. She did not even fetch water then, finding it painful to answer the routine questions from the women. Yet, in a way, she had begun to love her painful isolation. She was preparing for her degree examination, studying Spinoza and Rousseau, and she read many other historians and philosophers whose names she did not know. Her world was becoming full of ideas with little academic discipline imposed on it. She was growing up in all directions like a wild weed. She looked forward to the time now when her father left for school, for then she was free to pursue her interests. She wrote short stories and poems about characters who lived in the street, and taught herself to read and write in Gurmukhi, and this opened up another literary world for her.

Although Asha cooked for her father her attitude to eating had taken a very strange turn. She had begun to loathe the act of eating and she was glad when her father accepted the excuse that she ate later and that she did not like to eat early in the morning. She enjoyed the supreme act of will she could impose on herself, and the complete mastery she had over her own body. She enjoyed denying it food. She decided to give it the same food every day; two chapattis, an aubergine and potato curry, then she reduced it to one chapatti, and then to only half.

When she reached that stage she no longer felt hungry. The monotony of the food and the eating ritual filled her with loathing, and she never touched any of the foods her mother had sent her. Instead she stealthily distributed the goodies to children or friends. In the summer she spent all her time reading or writing on the hard charpoy on the verandah, and in the winter when it grew very cold she found it hard to keep warm and changed her routine of food: she cut out all solid food except sweet tea and a chapatti soaked in it. By now her body was resenting this treatment: her long luxuriant hair fell out in great handfuls; she stopped having her periods; and was perpetually catching colds, coughs, sore throats and bouts of high temperature. She started having sores and boils and her weight fell to seventy pounds but she felt elated. She had complete mastery and control over herself: she could now walk away from her plate of food and not feel a thing.

But this ravaged condition masked many things – a feeling of rage, rejection, hatred and betrayal. She had continued to write to Theep at least once a week – telling him all about her life at Sarē Dubē, her undying love for him, and her parents' continued mortification and distress at seeing him going about his business in Sarē Marē. He could not reply to her as all her letters were censored by her father. At one time she offered to marry him if he would only leave the village and not continue to distress her poor mother. But she had little idea how her letters were received and read, and if they had any effect on Theep. But she kept on hearing from her father, 'That brazen-faced bastard is still in the village boasting about your infatuation for him! I would like to break his neck, the son of a bitch! And how you were ready to run away with him if he hadn't talked sense into you.'

'But that's not true, father.' But her father did not provide her with the opportunity or the encouragement for a full answer.

There was a boy who used to be coached by her father; he had a prominent nose and looked like Mister Punch. He would say to her, 'Look at your skinny arms! You can't possibly carry that bucket of water, let me.' Asha liked him but all the while images of Theep kept her mind and feelings preoccupied. It was by curious coincidence that she learnt of the intensity of Kumar's feelings for her. She had sent for a New Year diary for Theep from a well-known national magazine but she had made a mistake in filling in the postal order which was returned to the village post master along with her list of instructions as to whom the diary should be sent to. In these small communities the notion that a girl should be sending a gift to a man could turn into a scandal, particularly as Asha's family were well known and respected in the village. The post master now wished to contact Asha's father concerning the offending postal order with information about the diary being sent to Theep. But Kumar rescued the situation and confronted her with the postal order; he wanted an explanation as to why she was spending her father's hard-earned money on a diary for a Sikh boy, and had she also sent him the photographs she had asked him to take for her? She had asked Kumar to take some pictures with a box camera, and they were now with Theep. After this painful episode Kumar saw less and less of her; he took care to depart as soon as his lesson was over. But before the chill winter set in he came to see her. As usual she was unwell and was sleeping in the sun under a blanket. She found comfort in doing this on the days she was unwell, feverish and shivery; she would look through the blanket, and through each minute gap in the weave she could view the splendid magnification and the prismatic, colourful spheres of the sun, reflected in the endless pattern of a kaleidoscope. These most intricate webs of rainbow colours and their perpetual movement would soothe and comfort her; she would move into the realms of a hypnotic trance and forget her headaches and become wonderfully drowsy. Now Kumar was gently shaking her and she awoke with a start – the late morning sun was warm, she was no longer shivery.

Kumar told her that he was going away to study agriculture in a nearby university and he had come to beg leave of her. The meeting was brief and touching. Kumar touched her feet with his forehead and said that she was the only person he had loved and respected with all his heart, and there never would be another one to take her place. She was very moved; she cried for him and wished him well, told him to come back and see her during the holidays, told him how much she valued his friendship. But at this stage all her emotions were totally and irrevocably committed to Theep who in the long eighteen months had become her religion.

Asha was studying Shakespeare, particularly the tragedies. *Julius Caesar, Othello* and *Hamlet* were her favourites, and over and over again she created and recreated the melodramas, assumed the roles of Desdemona and Ophelia on an empty stage in a lonely, deserted house in a small village, and no one heard or saw her. The incongruities in her lifestyle were indeed countless. Her father said that she was capable of taking the Degree examination in one year after having performed so brilliantly in the Intermediate examination, and she had gone through the syllabus many times. So he entered her for the examination to be held at one of the centres in the city. She spent two weeks there sitting the various papers.

She stayed at her father's friend's house as the examination centre was nearby. It was very hot as April was coming to an end and a rickshaw came to collect her every day. During the second week the son of the family returned from the air force. He was delighted to find Asha, all alone, unchaperoned in the house and he made every effort to seduce her.

Twice he came into the bedroom in the middle of the night, and during the day he spent long hours reading her poems, holding her hand and gazing into her eyes. Asha found this immediate attention very disconcerting; she was under pressure yet she did not know how to cope with the situation. She could hardly inform her father as both Mander's father and her father were close friends. She had little idea and little experience of coping with this predicament. One day, Mander actually came into her bed, undid her bra, and started kissing and fondling her breasts; she struggled but did not make a noise as his father was sleeping in the room next door. Luckily the dog followed him into the room and started barking, and he left. She was full of hurt and rage the next day and did not eat anything; consequently she felt that she had performed badly in the political science examination papers. After the examinations she was glad to get back to Sarē Dubē, to her own anonymity and isolation.

In the latter part of the year she had struck up a friendship with a girl who was a year older than her and was confined more or less to a completely uneventful existence before she could be married off. She was very well developed, and on the plump side, and her father was a Hakim. Each time a prospective match was in sight, her father would start giving her large doses of purgatives, so that she could lose weight and look slim and sylph-like but she never did. She started visiting Asha, wanting her to write the occasional letter to a boy she had a crush on, but later she took the role of feeding Asha and generally nurturing her. On the off days when Asha stayed in bed Kamla came beside her and held her, hugged her and then she would remove her shirt and let Asha nuzzle beside her ample bosoms.

Asha was extremely grateful for the warmth. She liked Kamla's breasts, they were beautiful and comforting, and their soft roundedness was one of the few aesthetic memories she carried in her head. Sometimes Kamla asked her if she would like to suckle her and Asha always did with a profound sense of gratitude, hunger and devotion. In those magic moments she was transported back again to a magical existence, an infant's secure world, free of pain, free of anxiety. She was grateful to Kamla for her comforting, generous nature and her gift of giving.

When her results came out, her father was beside himself with joy. She had topped the list for the district and had the highest marks in Political Science for the University. But Asha was happy too, for a different reason: she thought that her exile would end. She would be able to see her mother and taste her cooking. She missed the many tactile memories of her mother, the smell of her clothes, the touch of her stomach as she burrowed her nose into it and her reassuring, firm hands as she patted her and cupped her face in them. But disappointment was again around the corner. Asha was brought straight back to Sarē Dubē, the only difference being that Vijay had joined the high school, so now she had to mother Vijay and look after her father also. The household chores took longer and longer each day, and in her famished, self-starved condition she experienced extreme fatigue, spells of dizziness, nausea and headaches.

Kamla was still a regular visitor while other girls and women continued to make up fantasy stories about Asha never going back to her mother's. They varied from her having become pregnant and having an abortion, to elopement and many other lurid variations. Asha neither refuted nor made any comments about these tales when Kamla confronted her over and over again with this false testimony.

She now had time on her hands and her father asked her if she would like to take sewing lessons. A widow had come to live in the village; she was a sewing teacher at a school in the city but had come back to the village to claim her inheritance – a small, narrow house made with unfired bricks and mud. She did not mix well with the other women but gave sewing lessons. Asha soon found out she had no aptitude for cutting and making up clothes, etc. But she liked to learn various embroidery stitches and was anxious to improve. She wished to master all these in a short space of time but the teacher, the proud owner of a treadle machine, was loath to pass on these skills to Asha in a hurry. If it rained she would make the excuse, 'The machine is damp today, come tomorrow', and so on. But Asha loved turning pretty bits of velvet into flowers and plants, stems and stamens. But this uneasy partnership was soon terminated by the teacher when she found Asha far too industrious, inquisitive and willing.

The only other avenue left for Asha now was to take religion. She already accepted the fact that she was a sinner so she made a commitment to God. On most days she went with Kamla and joined a prayer and devotional songs group and sang, prayed and fasted most devotedly, asking God to forgive her sins, to eliminate all longing, desire and needs, and to make her like everyone else – a good person. For she believed most sincerely that all the girls of her age were good and pious while she alone had longings and desires which were damning in their intensity and content. She wished her mind to be washed pure of all things physical, of pride and arrogance, and be taught the path of humility and true obedience to the role in life – in other words to serve others. This devotion continued for most of the summer months; in the autumn there was to be a big gathering in a temple in the nearby town. Asha went there barefoot – so that her journey would be acceptable to God – accompanied by Kamla.

The hall was full of women of all ages, from young girls in arms to very old women who were feeble and unsteady on their feet. A very high altar with steps leading to it was ornately decked with flowers. On it, flanked by large cushions and antimacassars, lay a fat young priest supporting a white dhoti. He had a bald, shaved head and was garlanded with rows and rows of marigolds. Women crawled on their stomachs to pay him homage and kiss his feet, declaring their love for God and their sense of humility. Many devotional songs were sung and at the end of each song victory was hailed to the Great Guru. In her vulnerable and confused state Asha too was propelled forward. Her inadequacies and her weaknesses, her ego and pride overwhelmed her, and she bowed before the exalted feet of the Great Guru. With her head humbly bowed and eyes closed she listened to his great sermon which went as follows: 'You women who are gathered here today, and have chosen to serve God through *Us* in your wisdom, must remember that you are the symbol of original sin and weakness. It is because of you that the Gods and Saints were misled from their righteous path and began to serve Mammon and you. The Vedas in their wisdom have given you twenty-five years in a man's life, to serve him, to bear children to him and to obey him so that his name perpetuates, but then men must also abandon you to follow the path of God. Although you are weak and sinful and lead man astray from God, today, in his name, I am ready to bless you so that you can partake of this bounty.'

So overwhelmed was Asha with this instant vision of redemption that she fell at his feet and cried her eyes out for Nirvana. But soon, when the mass hysteria died down, she hated herself for being duped so easily. Religion now seemed utterly devoid of comfort and solace, and the mockery of it was the fat man sitting on the throne whose feet she had kissed so earnestly and reverently only a few moments ago. Her aloneness confronted her.

She walked away from the temple with her head held high promising herself never to give in to mass hysteria and organised religion, and that she must remember its hollowness which then sounded to her like a thousand clanging cymbals deafening her ears for a long time to come.

After taking care of Vijay and her father, Asha's days were the same, monotonous, long and uninspiring. No one came to see her and she called on no one. She waited for her family to decide her fate, although she had let them know very definitely that marriage was out. She would have to be sent to a teacher training college or to England where her sister was already working. Her sister had sent her an introduction to write to someone in England. This was a businessman, an Englishman in his fifties who was a close friend of her sister's. It gave her mind an avenue to express itself and she wrote to him regularly. The weekly letters were a catharsis from the suffocating existence she was leading. From him she learnt further about the glories of English country life, of fox hunting, of country fairs, of horse riding and races and of Kipling. He professed to be related to Kipling and had an old colonial's love of India. He believed in the British Empire with all its trappings and old glory. He also agreed to be her guardian as she was under age, and to ensure that she got a good education. There was a ray of hope, of optimism and freedom.

The date was set for her to fly to Britain in June; it was now the end of March. Her appetite had not returned, her wrists were painfully thin and she could see all the veins in her hands. But somehow this skeletal body made her feel spiritual. Then in May she was told that she was going to Sarē Marē.

She saw her mother who embraced her and cried at her pallid complexion and her thinness. Her sister too was pleased to see her but Asha somehow stayed strangely alone and apart. She had lost the way of coming back to her people. In her suffering, in her guilt and atonement, she had also removed herself from her mother.

She went upstairs as usual and from the corner of her eye she saw Theep indulging in the same old antics – the ones that used to move her so much, the ones that used to set her body and soul on fire.

Now all was ashes; the aversion therapy was complete. He now seemed a pathetic clown, a bumbling idiot who had already used up his bag of tricks. Asha turned her face away, the magic had gone out of her life, and with a heavy heart she walked slowly down the stairs, one step at a time. Theep too had joined the world of strangers.

When the day came for her to leave she knew that she was leaving the world of Sarē Dubē and Sarē Marē and her parents behind for good. With it she had also tried to leave the world of guilt, the confused and tortured sexuality, and her sense of individualism which had given her so much pain and had made her unfit for her motherland.

The road was long and dusty. She refused to let her father carry her case. Her mother stood, tearful, waiting by the roadside, but Asha never once looked back, and with each little step she felt she was removing herself from the shackles that bound her. She had also saved her most precious possession that her parents needlessly worried about – her virginity. She was a Traveller looking for Freedom and Love.